IT
TAKES
TWO

Kimberly Raymer

Zebra Books
Kensington Publishing Corp.

http://www.zebrabooks.com

To my parents, who have always been there for me, no matter what. My father, George F. Bowden, master of all things nautical, and my mother, Geraldine Pettit Bowden, who is above all else, my friend.

To my grandmother, Mildred Budd Bowden, who has always loved me unconditionally and who let me make mudpies.

ZEBRA BOOKS are published by

Kensington Publishing Corp.
850 Third Avenue
New York, NY 10022

First Printing: March, 1999
10 9 8 7 6 5 4 3 2 1

Printed in the United States of America

One

They were everywhere. Stapled to telephone poles, taped to windows, tacked on the bulletin board— bright fluorescent pink index cards had magically appeared sometime during the night, somewhat brightening the drab neighborhood where Lacey Campbell was temporarily staying. She had counted at least twenty of the cards on her walk from her motel room to the laundromat. Throwing down her duffel bag of dirty clothes and tucking the morning newspaper under her arm, she was drawn to the bulletin board to read the bold black print.

WANTED: SAILING PARTNER FOR LOCAL RACE. MUST BE EXPERIENCED SAILOR. WILL PAY $2000.00. CALL 555-8210.

She plucked the card off the bulletin board and frowned. This was too good to be true. She had taken sailing lessons once. She knew how to heave to and tack and a few other techniques of basic sailing, and she knew port from starboard. It wasn't exactly the same as running a fully staffed kitchen as she had done for the last eight years, but then it would beat waiting tables in a micro-mini skirt, the only other job she was qualified to do. And this definitely would be better than calling her mother and letting her and everyone in the family know she had failed at yet another thing in her life.

Lacey had convinced them all that taking the dream job as kitchen manager for the Palm Beach Fleming Inn, three thousand miles from Seattle, was a great career move and something she truly wanted. What she really wanted was to get as far away as possible from her ex-fiancé, Frank, and her stepsister, Jodi. The newlyweds. No need to let everyone know that her dream job had become yet another nightmare, or that she had quit only three weeks after accepting the position. She had managed to go from sleepless in Seattle, to penniless in Palm Beach, in one momentous month.

She dropped four quarters into the washing machine and started a load before sauntering over to the pay phone. Two thousand dollars was two thousand dollars, no matter how you looked at it, and she could certainly use the money. Two thousand would give her time to regroup, and rethink her situation without involving her family in any way.

She dialed the number from the index card and waited patiently through four rings. On the next ring, an answering machine came on with the cryptic message, "Interviews tonight at the Jolly Roger from 6 o'clock until position filled." That was it. She hung up and sighed. The masculine voice on the machine had sounded cold and intimidating. She flopped down into one of the plastic chairs and opened the newspaper. Six o'clock. She had about ten hours to kill.

* * *

Lacey slumped on her barstool. There had been people crowding around the table in the corner for over two hours, and she was sure the cushy sailing job had been filled by now. She sipped her mineral water and gave another sidelong glance at the corner table. Too many people were applying and she didn't feel like being charmingly competitive right now. She leaned her chin into her hands and sighed.

At the core of all her anguish was the feeling that maybe there was something terribly wrong with her. Her ex-fiancé hadn't been the first person to reject her. There had also been her father, but that was another story. Maybe she gave off bad vibrations.

"You want another water?" asked the bartender.

"No."

"That guy you're waiting to see is free now." He nodded towards the corner, whisking her glass away and wiping the bar.

Lacey could take a hint. She grabbed her purse and slid off the barstool. Taking a deep breath, she walked stiffly over to the man sitting at the corner table. When he looked up at her, she almost ran away. He was way too good-looking. For one thing, he had liquid brown puppy dog eyes. Eyes that would normally melt her heart, if she hadn't decided a few months earlier to give up on men. Plus he had a chin with a dimple and she was a sucker for chin dimples.

Preston Rockwell shifted his weight in his chair and leaned forward. Over one hundred people had shown up for interviews. One hundred of the city's Sunday sailors, losers, and college boys who'd dropped out after spring break. He had forgotten to mention on his cards that the sailing partner he so desperately needed had to be female. He felt his adrenaline start pumping as a pretty young woman with red hair in a long braid made her way towards him. Though he forced himself to fake a friendly smile, the woman still looked as if she might bolt at any minute.

He smiled wider. "Please sit down."

She slowly sank into the chair across from him, carefully draping her purse over the arm of the chair.

"Okay, it's like this," he began, trying not to sound as tense and impatient as he felt. "I had a partner for this race, but she backed out and I need a replacement, pronto."

The woman remained silent.

"I assume you have sailing knowledge and experience?" he asked.

The woman hesitated and he almost groaned aloud.

"I'm not exactly a seasoned sailor, but I have had lessons and I have sailed before," she said quietly.

Preston relaxed in his chair a little. "Where have you sailed?" he asked.

"Off the coast of Washington," she answered.

He brightened somewhat. "So you have been out on the ocean in a sailboat?"

She nodded.

"Have you ever raced?" he asked, knowing he was pushing his luck.

Lacey shook her head and he watched the long red braid swing behind her.

"Would you be able to get away for about two weeks starting Friday?"

"Friday?" she asked, her brows arching ever so slightly. He could feel the knots return to his stomach. "You mean I've got the job?"

Preston quickly nodded. "If you want it, it's yours."

"I want it," she said firmly, the tension leaving her face.

Preston tried to hide his excitement and relief. He wanted to hug her, to kiss her, to marry her. Instead he merely said, "We have to register tomorrow. The race starts Friday. We'll be racing around Bermuda."

"When would I get the money?" she asked.

He held down his disappointment. So that was all she was interested in. He knew the type well. "After the race."

"Even if we lose?" she asked.

Preston felt his face pale. "No problem." He gave her a weakened smile.

He shifted in his chair as the woman carefully studied him from across the table. At one time, he had total and complete confidence in his looks and his power over women, and such scrutiny would never have bothered him in the least. But that was in the past and he felt himself squirming uncomfortably under her direct gaze.

"Tell me more about the race," she said.

He cleared his throat and began. "Have you heard of the Ridgeway Yacht Club Race which is held here every other year?"

The woman shook her head. "I've only been in Palm Beach for about a month."

Preston tried not to let his relief show in his eyes or voice. "Well, every other year, ten sailboats race from Palm Beach around Bermuda and back, and the winner gets five thousand dollars." Actually the purse was much greater, but she didn't need to know that.

"You're going to a lot of trouble for only five thousand dollars," she remarked.

"There's a lot of prestige associated with winning the race," he answered tightly. He wasn't about to tell her he desperately needed the money.

"Why did your other partner drop out?" she asked, frowning.

"I'm not exactly sure," he answered tersely.

"You realize I'm not real experienced, don't you?" she asked, her frown wrinkling her forehead. "I don't want you blaming me if we lose."

"I'm experienced enough for both of us," he said carefully. "We'll have to register tomorrow morning. Only the first ten couples signing up can compete." He was beginning to feel uneasy about her, but time was running out to find a better partner on such short notice. "Do you happen to have a birth certificate with you here in Florida?"

She nodded, puzzled. "Why?"

"You'll need it to dock in Bermuda. Are you sure you'll sail with me?"

She tapped her fingernails on the table. He noticed they were sensible nails, not long, sculptured, or painted some garish color. What was she thinking? He held his breath.

She hesitated. "Do I need to buy anything for this trip?"

"No. All you need are your clothes. I'll provide the rest."

She looked relieved, yet still she hesitated, and panic gripped him as he felt his opportunity slip away.

"How about if I pay you twenty-five hundred dollars?" he added for good measure.

She took a deep breath. "Okay. But this is strictly business. I mean it. I know karate, and judo, and kickboxing, and I won't hesitate to use all of them," she said.

He refrained from pointing out that if she violently incapacitated him, she might find herself floundering at sea for the rest of her life. Instead he stuck out his hand. Reluctantly she put her hand in his and they shook.

"We've got a deal?" he asked.

"We've got a deal," she said reluctantly.

"I'll drive you to your motel," he offered generously.

"That's okay. I have a room right up the street."

"Good. Let me walk you there so I can find it tomorrow. I'll pick you up at four o'clock in the morning for our registration."

"Four o'clock? That's so early," she protested, glancing at her watch.

"I told you only the first ten couples registered can compete and I intend for us to be the first couple there."

They walked to her motel in silence and he left her at the door of her room.

"Hey!" she yelled at him.

He turned to her, praying she hadn't already changed her mind.

"I don't even know your name," she said.

"Preston Rockwell. What's yours?" he asked.

"Lacey Campbell. See you at four." She pushed open the door of her room and disappeared into the darkened interior.

"Mom, you told me to have fun. What could be more fun than crewing on a sailboat trip to Bermuda?" Lacey closed her eyes and massaged her forehead with her fingers. "They're letting me take my vacation time early, that's all." She lay back on the bed and flung out her arm, wishing she didn't have to lie. "I promise I'll let you know the details tomorrow. Yes, I love Palm Beach. Tell Tom I said hello."

She hung up and let out a heavy sigh. No way was she going to make her mother worry. She dragged her shoulder bag across the bed and dug for her wallet, carefully pulling the folded bills from their hidden compartment and counting them. She had exactly two hundred and sixty-three dollars left. Not enough for air fare to Washington state, not enough for a security deposit for an apartment, not enough to get herself out of the fix her pride had gotten her into.

Preston couldn't sleep. What if his new-found partner didn't show up tomorrow? What if the bank decided to foreclose on his mother's home before he could get back? What if he, God forbid, lost the race, and everything he owned. Unlike his father, he wasn't a gambler. His stomach had been doing flipflops ever since he had come up with this scheme.

His friend, Henry, had thought he was kidding, and had laughingly offered to trade Preston his sailboat for Preston's car, knowing the Rockwells' yacht had been sold months earlier. Preston had quickly agreed to the trade.

"I'm going to enter the race this year."

"Preston, you can't be serious," Henry had said, wide-eyed.

"I've never been more serious."

"You'll be up against seasoned sailors, people who've competed every year of the race. What makes you think you can win?"

"I've got to win," he had answered grimly. That was the bottom line. He had to win this race if he was going to save his mother's home.

Four o'clock found Lacey standing outside the motel, nibbling on a stale bagel she had saved from the day before. She was surprised she was so calm, considering she was about to embark on the only spontaneous thing she had ever done in her life. Even her move to Florida had been carefully thought out and planned, yet, nothing had prepared her for the deplorable working conditions in the posh hotel kitchen.

She was going to put all her energy into sailing to Bermuda and getting that money. She glanced at her watch again just as a set of headlights approached her. A sleek black sports car screeched to an abrupt stop. She peered carefully into the darkened interior before opening the door, sliding in, and fastening her seatbelt.

"You're late," she couldn't resist saying.

Preston grunted and pulled out of the parking lot with another screech.

"What kind of car is this?" She rubbed her hands over the leather upholstery.

"A Jaguar," Preston muttered as he took a corner on what felt like two wheels.

"Maybe I should raise my price," she said jokingly.

"What?" he snapped.

"Just joking. Guess you aren't a morning person."

She leaned back in her seat and closed her eyes, pretending not to mind his reckless driving. Finally the car skidded to a stop. Preston got out and began striding into the darkness. She struggled out of the car and jumped out to follow him.

"Hey, wait up! It's still dark out here." She stumbled on something and barely missed falling on her face. A strong hand righted her and she ungraciously mumbled her thanks.

"I'm sorry. I need coffee," Preston said, keeping a firm grasp on her arm and led her to the steps of a dark building. "Good. We're first." He sat on the steps and sighed. He'd kill for some coffee. Lacey settled beside him and they sat, tolerating each other in silence.

"Are we going to sit here for two hours?" she flatly asked.

Preston gave a long-suffering sigh. "I told you I need to be first."

"Why?"

"Because I want to make sure I'm in this race," he answered with a fierce intensity.

Lacey didn't reply. Instead she began fumbling with her purse and withdrew a sheet of motel stationery. She thrust it and a pen at him. "I need you to sign this."

Preston took the paper and squinted at it in the poor light. "What is it?"

She fumbled in her purse again and emerged with a book of matches from the Jolly Roger. "It's a contract." She lit a match and held it up so Preston could read the carefully written words. "It says you agree to pay me twenty-five hundred dollars if I sail with you to Bermuda as a crew member."

A soft breeze blew out the match just before it burned her fingers, and she lit another one.

"Sign there." She pointed to a line drawn at the bottom of the paper.

They sat in silence for over an hour before two more cars drove up, and they could hear the chatter of voices and several car doors slamming. As the voices drew closer, Lacey could see another couple and two men in the half light. The men stopped at the bottom step and peered at Preston.

"Preston? You're really going to race this year? I thought it was another rumor," the taller man said.

"No. I'm racing."

"Where are you getting a sailboat?"

"Henry Reese is trading me his boat for my car."

The men looked at each other. "What about the entry fee? It's pretty steep," the taller one said again. The other couple stood awkwardly behind the men, and Lacey detected tension so thick it was tangible.

"Look, I'm here to register with my partner, and my money is just as good as the next guy's, isn't it? I believe I am still an official yacht club member, am I not?"

The shorter man shrugged and started up the steps. "It's your money."

The taller man followed, shaking his head. They opened the building and turned on the lights. It was the first chance Lacey had to see Preston's face clearly and she was surprised to see how vulnerable he looked, despite his gruffness.

"What's going on?" she asked him quietly.

He looked at her as if he just remembered her presence. Suddenly the gruffness was back and the tiny twinge of pity she had begun to feel for him quickly evaporated with his next words. "Don't worry your pretty little head about anything but being on that boat Thursday night." He entered the building with her close on his heels, and they spent ten minutes filling out forms.

The taller man took the forms and read them carefully, studying Lacey over the rim of his reading glasses. "She's not a member of the yacht club," he stated.

"Show me the rule that says she has to be a member." Preston leaned on the table with both hands.

The men looked at each other again. "Okay. Where's your entry fee?"

Preston stood up and looked at Lacey. He handed her two dollars. "Could you run across the street and get us a cup of coffee? The store's probably open by now."

She yanked the money from his hand and walked angrily out the door and to the small store across the street. Did he think she was going to run errands and be his servant for the next two weeks? She bought the coffee for him, but didn't get any for herself. She almost ran into him as she was leaving the store. "Oh. Is that it?" she asked.

"That's it. I'll take you back to the motel now."

"Wait a minute." Lacey handed Preston his styrofoam cup full of coffee and went over to the pay phone outside the convenience store. She inserted some change and rapidly dialed a number. The change was promptly returned to her. "Yes, collect from Lacey."

She looked at him staring at her while she waited for her mother to answer the phone. It would be only three a.m. in Seattle, but she knew her mother would want this opportunity to quiz the captain of her sailing trip to Bermuda.

"Mom. I'm sorry to wake you, but I wanted you to talk to the guy I'm sailing to Bermuda with and let him explain our plans to you." She handed the phone to Preston as a spray of coffee erupted from his mouth and rained over his shoes and the parking lot. He put his cup down on the sidewalk and held his hand over the mouthpiece.

"What in the hell am I suppose to say to your mother?" he hissed.

"Convince her you're safe or she'll worry about me." Lacey shrugged.

Preston hesitated before speaking into the phone. "Hello?"

What followed was the grilling of his life. When he hung up, he heaved a sigh of relief. "Your mother knows more about me than my mother. You Campbells sure are a trusting bunch."

"If I disappear, she'll know where to start looking. Besides, would you trust you?" she retorted.

Preston looked as if she had hit him. Finally he shook his head. "No, I guess not," he said gruffly. "Let's go."

He stalked angrily across the street with Lacey following, wondering what she had said to make him so angry. As he opened his car door, a car skidded to a halt next to him, scattering gravel against the Jaguar.

"Rockwell! Surprised to see you here." Rodney Fleming jumped out and stopped upon seeing Lacey standing stiffly by Preston's car. "Ms. Campbell." He gave her a curt nod.

Preston turned to see Lacey's face first turn pale and then red.

"Mr. Fleming," she bit out between clenched teeth.

"You two know each other?" Preston asked suspiciously.

Rodney forced a laugh. "More than I want to, I'm afraid."

Lacey wrenched open the door of the car and got in with a slam. She sat breathing heavily, listening to the muted conversation between the two men who obviously hated one another.

"Where'd you get the entry money? A bank robbery?" said Rodney with a sneer.

Preston clenched his fists. "You had better get going if you want to register in time."

Rodney looked over to see a line of five couples. He looked quickly at his watch. "I hope Cynthia won't be late." He looked up as if remembering something, and smiled. "She seemed to think you somehow expected her to race with you. Now why would she think that?"

"Because I asked her, maybe?" answered Preston sarcastically.

"She said if she thought you really could have come up with the ten thousand dollar entry fee, she might have been tempted," Rodney continued.

Preston glanced down nervously to make sure the Jaguar windows were rolled up. Lacey Campbell didn't need to know how much the race entry fee was, as it would only make her ask more questions. He looked back up to see Cynthia's convertible pull into the lot.

"Gotta go. Good luck." Rodney laughed as he went to claim the golden blonde who was getting out of the car. Preston opened the door and got into the Jaguar with a slam that rivaled Lacey's.

"How long have you known Fleming?" he demanded.

"I worked for him and his father for about eight years at the Seattle Fleming Inn. He happens to be the reason I moved to Florida."

Preston sat silently gripping the steering wheel. "How do I know this isn't a set-up?"

Lacey turned to him, frowning. "What?"

"You. Maybe Rodney paid you to sabotage my chances of winning the race."

She gave him a withering look. "Yes, you're right. You caught me. I confess. He sent me to the bar where he knew you'd go looking for a partner at the very last minute for this race. Oh, and when we get out to sea, I'm to supposed drill holes in the bottom of your boat. Really, Mr. Rockwell, if you weren't so self-involved, you would have noticed that I don't particularly care for Mr. Fleming myself. Now take me to my motel. The deal is off. Find a female you can trust." She flung herself back in her seat and crossed her arms, determinedly facing the tinted window.

Preston threw the car in gear and drove with breakneck speed to Lacey's motel. He skidded to a halt in the parking lot and turned off the motor. Lacey fumbled with her seat belt and threw open the car door.

"Wait." Preston grabbed her arm. "I'm sorry. I've had a very tense few weeks."

She glared at him. "Did it ever occur to you that maybe I've had a few tense weeks myself? Did you for even one minute stop and think that I must be pretty darn desperate to take on a hare-brained sailing race when I don't know the first thing about you or even about sailing?" She was breathing heavily, her cheeks bright pink.

"I said I'm sorry." He needed this obstinate female to win and he wasn't used to begging.

She sat glaring at him. "Why on earth would you pay ten thousand dollars just to win five thousand?" she finally asked.

Preston looked away. "For the prestige of winning the race, remember?"

"Then if you don't need the money, I want the full five thousand if I'm to go with you."

Preston turned to glare at her. The little con artist. She had him by the unmentionables, and she knew it. "Fine. You get all five thousand—if we win, but only twenty-five hundred if we lose," he snapped. Two weeks stuck on a boat wanting to kill the only human nearby would definitely be a good character builder for him, he decided.

She pulled the contract out of her purse and neatly printed in the amount of five thousand dollars to be given to her by Preston with the stipulation that they win the race. "Initial this. I'm mailing it to my mother for safekeeping." Preston yanked the paper from her hand and initialed it so hard the pen went through the paper, leaving an ink blotch on his khaki pants. She carefully wrote her initials next to his and folded the contract and slid it into an envelope.

She looked up. "Now what?"

"I pick you up tonight at eight sharp, we spend the night on the boat, and set sail at six tomorrow morning." He stared steadfastly out the car window.

"Fine. See you then." She slammed the car door with a vengeance and Preston watched as she twitched her little behind angrily through the door of the motel lobby. If she wasn't so pushy and demanding, and if he wasn't so embroiled in a family crisis, this might have been fun. He always liked a challenge where women were concerned and Lacey Campbell certainly seemed like a challenge.

Two

Lacey stood stiffly inside the motel lobby and watched Preston drive away. Looking down at her watch, she determined she'd save some money if she checked out of the motel before eleven. No need to pay for a night and not sleep here. She walked rapidly to her room and lost no time in showering. Then she spent the rest of the morning switching clothes around in her four stuffed suitcases. There was no way she was going to take all of her luggage on the boat, so she decided to take the suitcases to the local bus station and store them in a locker. After several attempts to carry all four bags, she reluctantly called a cab to take her the five blocks to the bus station.

Forty-five minutes later, she had rented a locker and pushed all but her duffel bag inside; that she threw over her shoulder and lugged with her up the tourist-packed streets of Palm Beach. She stopped in the first discount drugstore she saw and bought three bottles of sunscreen. She had gotten a hellacious sunburn once and with her fair skin, she never wanted to go through the pain and blisters again. She also bought a cheap pair of sunglasses and a large spray can of insect repellent, just in case. She considered buying some mace in case Preston got out of hand.

Lacey headed for the public library and settled her

purchases and duffel bag at one of the tables. The friendly librarian helped her locate several books on sailing and Bermuda, which she began studying with relish. It was a relief to sit down. Her stuff had begun to weigh a ton on the walk from the drug store and she hoped she could relax for awhile before being in Preston Rockwell's disturbing presence.

She began reading the first book on sailing. All the sailing terminology sounded so complicated and she was suddenly relieved that Preston Rockwell hadn't seemed worried about her inexperience. She wondered if he was buying everything they needed for the boat, and if he had the required flares, life preservers, emergency raft, and other necessary supplies recommended by the book. She eventually nestled her head in her arms on the table and closed her eyes.

Preston slowly dialed Aunt Doreen's number. Over six months ago he had sent his mother to visit his father's sister in Virginia, and though Aunt Doreen knew what was going on, his mother was still living in blissful ignorance. He had to make sure she didn't try to call him or come home in the next two weeks, when he wouldn't be around to protect her from her so-called friends. He had never noticed before how his social set thrived on the misfortunes of others.

"Hi, Aunt Doreen. It's Preston."

His aunt's raspy voice barked over the line, "Are things straight yet? Geraldine's getting antsy to get back home."

"That's why I'm calling. To give her a reason to stay at least a month longer. How is she?" His mother would never know the lengths he had gone to in the last six months to keep her in blissful ignorance.

Aunt Doreen hesitated. "She's still wondering why your father killed himself. She thinks it must somehow be her fault, or he was deathly ill with some disease." Suddenly her voice took on a fierce strength. "And you, you damn fool, are keeping everything from her. The truth might hurt her, Preston, but it also might help her heal."

Preston took a determined breath. "I'm doing what's best. Could I talk to her?"

"Hold on." He heard the phone clatter and his aunt's voice fading in the background. He would never tell his mother the truth. It wasn't necessary because he thought she couldn't handle the truth—it was more that he knew he couldn't handle telling it to her.

"Preston?"

"Mom. I wanted to call and let you know that Henry and I are sailing to Bermuda for a couple of weeks." He waited, hoping she wouldn't remember the annual Yacht Club race.

"But I was hoping to come home Sunday."

Taking a calculated risk, Preston said, "Well, come on, but I won't be here."

"Well . . . I guess I could stay on. Aunt Doreen isn't driving me totally crazy—yet." He could hear her hesitation. "Are you still dating Cynthia?"

Preston grimaced into the phone. "Yes. She sends her love," he lied. Lying was beginning to come naturally to him, and he wondered if being an adept liar was a trait he had inherited from his father.

"Good. It's time you settled down, son."

It was an old conversation. Her desire for a grandchild had been a litany in their house since he was old enough to reproduce. Thank heavens he hadn't yet. What awful traits would his children inherit?

"I'll call you when we get back and you can have Aunt Doreen bring you down."

"Okay. I love you, son. Please be careful. I don't know what I'd do . . ." She left the sentence unfinished.

"Mom, I'll be fine. I love you." He hung up and stretched across the unmade bed. It had been a tense two days, and he had gotten little sleep. In fact, ever since the day the police had entered the door of the posh Rockwell Investment Counseling office almost seven months ago, telling him his father's body had been found in the silver Mercedes parked on the beach, dead from an apparently self-inflicted gunshot, he had not had one good night's sleep.

When the bills began trickling in, he realized that for his father, suicide apparently was the easier route than facing the consequences of his gambling. The old man had loved the good life, but Preston found it hard to understand, let alone forgive, his father for gambling away everything they owned.

Hardest of all to forgive was that his father had left Preston's mother on the verge of homelessness, because there was a $100,000.00 note due on the house in less than two months. And it wasn't just that the man had borrowed against their ancestral home, but that it was in reality Preston's mother's estate; the home where she was born and raised, and her father before her, his father before him. His father had no right to gamble away what wasn't even his.

Though Preston had sold everything from the family yacht to the antique furniture he was sure his mother would never miss from the rambling rooms of the estate, and had let all their staff go, nothing had put a dent into the magnificent debt bequeathed to him by his father.

He hoped his sailing partner, Lacey, was waiting for him as she had promised. If he could just win the race, get the prize money, pay the remaining debts, and put the shattered pieces of his life back together . . . He closed his eyes and drifted off into an exhausted sleep.

"Miss." A persistent push on Lacey's shoulder nudged her slowly awake. It took her several seconds to realize where she was.

"Miss. We close at six. I'm sorry, but you'll have to leave." The librarian was standing over her apologetically.

Lacey blinked several times before focusing on her watch and stretching. She had slept almost two hours and she was hungry. She hurriedly returned the books to their shelves and lugged her duffel bag outside as the librarian locked the doors behind her. She walked across the street to a hole-in-the-wall restaurant and grabbed a greasy burger.

After almost swallowing it whole, she went into a secondhand book store and bought a how-to book on sailing since she hadn't gained much knowledge in the library. Looking again at her watch, she figured she might as well return to the motel parking lot, though she still had almost an hour to wait for Preston.

When she walked past the motel sign she immediately spotted the Jaguar, and next to it slumped Preston, sitting on the curb, his head in his hands. She walked up to him.

"Hey. You're early," she said as Preston looked up, his face pale. "What's wrong?" He looked so pathetic she felt another twinge of pity, which he rapidly dispelled with his ferocious attack.

"Where in the hell have you been?" he asked between clenched teeth.

She held up her bags. "Shopping. Why?"

"I came for you over two hours ago and they told me you had checked out. Then I traced you with the cab company to the bus station, and there your trail disappeared."

"Well, I can't afford to pay for a motel room I won't be using, and where else could I leave all my luggage but a bus station? Besides, you said eight and it's only ten after seven. What's the problem?"

"The problem is I thought you had quit on me, dammit." His eyes were bloodshot and red, and if Lacey didn't know better, she would think he had been crying. But that was silly, because people like Preston had nothing to cry about.

"Well, I didn't, and I think you're upset for no reason. If anything, you should be glad I'm early." She sat beside him on the curb, and looked at him. "Why wouldn't I show up? We have a written contract, remember?"

"I don't know why you wouldn't show up." They sat in silence for a few minutes until Lacey could stand it no longer.

"This race means a lot to you, doesn't it?" she asked quietly.

"Yes. It means everything," Preston answered.

"Does it have anything to do with the blonde who was meeting Fleming?"

Preston looked at her sharply. "Why?"

"Because I heard him say she almost sailed with you instead. Is she the one who dumped you?"

"Yes," he said bitterly.

Poor Preston. She knew all too well the pain of being dumped, especially for another person. That was two strikes against Rodney Fleming. First for ignoring her complaints against the unsafe kitchen at his posh hotel, and second, for causing that blonde to dump Preston. She stood up abruptly and grabbed her bags. "Let's go."

He stood up and went over to open the trunk. Before he could help her with the bags, she threw them in and was yanking open the car door. He flinched as she slammed it shut. He softly closed the trunk and peered through the open driver's window.

"Are you all right?" he asked.

"I'm fine. Let's go."

Preston got into the car and started the engine. "I didn't say anything to upset you, did I?" he asked.

Lacey smiled at him. "Of course not. I just want to get used to the feel of the boat. Who knows? I may be violently seasick the whole trip."

He gathered speed and drove with reckless abandon towards the wharf.

"I certainly hope you know how to sail better than you know how to drive," she commented through clenched teeth.

He screeched to a halt. "What's wrong with my driving?"

"Oh, nothing. I'm sure the three pedestrians you

almost hit at the last intersection think you drive divinely."

"Are you going to be carping at me this whole trip?" Preston got out of the car and stood looking at her impatiently.

"Maybe. I have a feeling I'll have a lot to carp about." She got out and slammed the door. "What kind of food did you buy?"

Preston looked at her blankly. "Food?"

Lacey put her hands impatiently on her hips. "You know, the stuff you eat?"

Preston paled. "I forgot to get food."

"Well, go get some. I'll unpack my things."

His face flushed. "I can't."

"What do you mean you can't?" she said. "I'm not sailing to Bermuda without food."

"I don't have any money with me."

"Use your Visa Gold card or Master Card or American Express, then. We need supplies."

"I left my charge cards home," he lied, not wanting her to know they had all been canceled months ago.

"You rich people sure are helpless," she said. "I'll pay for the groceries, but you owe me whatever I spend. Got it?"

"Agreed. I'm sorry. Look, you take the car and go get the groceries, and I'll wait for my friend, Henry. He's coming down to explain where everything is on the boat." He threw her the car keys.

"Are you sure you trust me to take your car?" she asked in wonder, deftly catching the keys.

"Yes," he answered tersely before turning and walking down the pier. He felt like a complete and utter fool, and for some reason he didn't like the fact that the girl was probably feeling the same way about him. But he wasn't used to planning ahead. In the past, it had all been done for him. He cringed when he heard the tires spin out of the gravel parking lot.

Lacey climbed into the Jaguar and deliberately spun out of the gravel parking lot. Food, for heaven's sake. Everyone had to eat. Wondering what else he had forgotten, she made a mental note to thoroughly check out the boat for emergency supplies as soon as she boarded. She turned into the grocery store parking lot, thankful she had remembered her way there.

She wheeled a cart into the store and carefully cruised the aisles, wishing she had looked at the kitchen of the boat first. She had no idea of what the accommodations for food were. She bought tea bags and instant coffee, but got decaffeinated. Preston certainly didn't need any caffeine—he was jumpy and moody enough. She hurried through the store, throwing items into her cart with abandon. After she paid the cashier, she loaded her purchases in the trunk and carefully folded the cash register receipt and stored it in her wallet before getting into the car and driving hurriedly back to the wharf. After she parked and grabbed two of the bags, she stopped and stared down the long pier.

In the semi-darkness, all the sailboats looked alike, their lights twinkling like stars in the darkness. Which boat was Preston's? She sighed and put the bags back in the trunk and started walking down the pier. The sailboats were all rather large and had names which verged on unbearably cute, like the *Filthy Rich, Party Animal, All Hours, For Sail, The Stud Muffin,* and the like. But none said *Nincompoop,* or *Stupid Rich Boy,* so there was no clue as to Preston's location.

She went back to the car and honked the horn three times, but no one even came out onto the boat decks to look. She finally walked halfway down the pier and screamed Preston's name at the top of her lungs.

Several heads came up at her scream and she saw a flustered Preston rushing out of a boat not far from where she stood.

"What are you doing?" he said, clamping his hand on her arm.

"I'm trying to find you. I've got bags of groceries and you didn't tell me which boat is ours."

"Mine. Not ours." He held out his hand. "Give me the keys, and I'll bring in the groceries." Lacey handed him the keys and shook her arm free from his grasp, rubbing where his fingers had been. He stalked up the pier and opened the trunk with her close on his heels.

"Good God! What did you buy?" he asked in horror when he saw all the bags.

She reached around him and grabbed her duffel bag and the two bags from her afternoon shopping trip. "More than you thought to buy, Mr. Wonderful." She spun around and walked angrily down the pier, while Preston struggled with the jugs of water she had bought.

She located the boat he had emerged from, and stepped carefully across the plank leading down to the deck. When she jumped down from the plank, the boat barely rocked, which was a vast relief. She got dizzy on carnival rides, so she wasn't at all sure how well she'd handle a long sea voyage.

She walked down the narrow three steps into the dimly lit cabin and cringed at the closeness of everything. The kitchen area was jammed almost into the bunks, and she wondered how in the world she'd survive two weeks with Preston Rockwell in such a small space.

She threw her bags onto the bunk on the right and walked towards the kitchen. There was a two-burner stove, a tiny sink, and a secured ice chest, with no ice. She supposed Preston hadn't thought of that, either. She sighed as Preston lugged down the first load of groceries.

"I guess I'll have to go buy ice, too," she said angrily.

"No. Henry already went to get us some." He dropped the groceries into the sink and on the stove. "Since I'll be doing the sailing, you can have galley duty, starting with putting this stuff away."

"Fine by me." Lacey started storing away the food in large bins secured with small bungee cords as Preston left the cabin. She sighed with relief at his exit. This boat was entirely too small.

After two more trips to the car, Preston finished bringing in the groceries, and returned onto deck to wait for his friend Henry, not comfortable with Lacey flitting around the cabin, opening and slamming doors, and generally being a pest with her questions.

The first thing she asked was how to work the toilet, so he had to explain it to her.

"You have to hold down this pedal at the bottom with your foot until sea water fills the toilet," he had explained patiently. "And then pump this handle on the wall about fourteen times, and everything will disappear into the ocean."

"Ugh. Poor fish."

"And be sure not to put anything in here that might clog the lines."

"I think I can manage to avoid that," she said sarcastically.

Next he had to assure her there were emergency flares, plenty of propane for the stove, an emergency life raft, a life preserver that she apparently thought was vital, life jackets, and a fully packed first aid kit.

She made him feel so damn inadequate, thinking of all the things that had never occurred to him before Henry's patient lecture earlier that evening. Henry had always been a serious sailor, but in Preston's previous sailing experiences, his only concern had been the woman he was with, not the boring mundane details. Sailing used to be fun.

He heard Henry walking up the pier before he saw him.

"Give me a hand with this, will you?" Henry called to him.

Preston jumped down and helped Henry lift the huge bag of ice onto the boat. They took it down and placed it in the cooler, when Henry noticed Lacey, pressed against the door to the head.

"Well, hello," Henry said appreciatively, arching his eyebrows at Preston. "Too bad this is a race, Pres."

Preston cleared his throat in warning and quickly steered his friend back on deck. "Don't get her riled up, Henry. Didn't you notice the red hair?"

"Yeah, among other things. Where did you find her again?"

"Never mind. Here." Preston thrust the keys to the Jaguar at him. "Thanks for the trade, buddy, and for lending me half the entry fee."

"No problem. Just win so we can thumb our noses at Fleming and Cynthia. I still can't believe she's sailing with that jerk."

"Well, that's our Cynthia . . . she wants to be with a winner. I just hope she's wrong."

"Hey, I've got something for you in my car." Henry leaped off the boat and sprinted up the pier, returning a moment later with a bottle of Dom Perignon which he thrust towards Preston. "This is for when you win."

"Thanks, Henry, for everything." They shook hands and Preston soon heard the roar of the Jaguar's engine. He walked down into the cabin and placed the champagne on his bunk, which he assumed was on the left, since there were items scattered all over the one on the right. Lacey was standing at the stove over a steaming frying pan.

"What are you doing?" he asked curiously, walking gingerly up behind her.

"Cooking myself some dinner. You want some?" she asked ungraciously.

"No, I'm not hungry."

She glanced at him before turning her attention back to the pan of sizzling mystery meat. "Is that smart?"

"What do you mean?" he gritted.

"I mean you've got to eat to have enough energy to sail this boat to Bermuda and back. Skipping meals is unhealthy."

"Thanks, but you don't need to mother me. I have a mother."

Lacey put a pan on the other burner and melted some shortening before turning to him, hands on her hips, apparently a pose she assumed when indignant. "Look, Mr. Rockwell, my life for the next two weeks is in your not too capable hands, from what I've seen. I have the right to demand certain things from you, such as that you remain healthy throughout this trip. Furthermore—"

He held up his hands in surrender. "Okay, okay. I'm sorry. It's just . . ."

"That you've had a few tense weeks," she finished for him, turning her attention once again to the stove. "I know, but so have I, and I don't feel like having anything else in my life mess up right now. If you'll leave the kitchen, I'll fix us both dinner."

"Galley."

Lacey turned to him. "What?"

"It's not a kitchen, it's a galley, and the bathroom is called the head."

"Thanks. Now how do you say 'get out of here before I scream' in boat talk?"

"Scuttle-butt," he answered quickly.

"Then scuttle-butt, or I'll burn your omelet." When he left the cabin, she was expertly breaking eggs into a bowl with one hand.

Three

Preston leaned back against the low outside cabin wall and sighed. Dinner had been delicious, and exactly what he had needed. If Lacey could cook this well using the limited equipment in the galley, she'd be worth the five thousand dollars he had promised to pay her if they won. He slanted a glance towards her silhouette, lit dimly by the lights from the pier and surrounding boats. He had purposely killed the outside lights of his craft to help isolate himself in darkness.

Lacey's endless questions were wearing him out, and if he hadn't been afraid of getting her started again, he would have complimented her on the fruit salad, fluffy omelet, and pan-fried mystery meat. Already, she had pointed out that the sheets on the bunks were damp and full of mildew, that there were only two saucepans, and one frying pan on board, and that there was no toilet paper, except the roll in the head, or rather half a roll.

He watched her stand up and stretch before returning to the cabin, and wondered if she were going to explode, having not spoken a word in over twenty minutes.

"There's no dish detergent, either," came an exasperated voice from the cabin door. "Are you absolutely sure you have flares, and life jackets, and flash-lights with batteries in them?''

Damn. Was she overly efficient, or was he really the inept clod that he apparently appeared to be? ''Just leave the dishes. I'll wash them.''

''With what? The sliver of soap stuck to the sink? If the race begins at six, we should be getting to sleep soon, and you doing dishes in that tiny kitchen later won't help me get any rest.''

''Galley,'' he said automatically.

''Whatever. We need more supplies before we set sail.''

''I'll take care of everything. Quit nagging me,'' he bellowed, surprising them both.

Lacey stood peering at him in the darkness before stomping below and slamming shut the cabin door. He was tempted to throw his plate and utensils over-board rather than to go into the cabin and face her, but he compromised by hiding them in the live bait well. He jumped gingerly off the boat and went to the pay phone at the end of the pier and called Henry. Luckily his friend was home, and agreed to bring the needed supplies and leave them on deck during the night, so Lacey wouldn't know. Preston hung up the phone feeling pretty proud of the way he'd taken care of the situation.

Lacey unhooked the storage locker under her bunk and stuffed in her empty duffel bag on the side of her tiny pile of clothes. To her chagrin, when she had unpacked earlier, she had discovered that she hadn't packed a thing to sleep in. She had remem-bered her toothbrush, her dental floss, even her hand cream, for God's sake, but she didn't have one thing to sleep in—not even an over-sized T-shirt.

She looked guiltily at the door of the cabin before quickly opening the locker under Preston's bunk, hoping he possessed a shirt of some kind for her to wear, only to find it completely empty. Puzzled, she hurriedly closed and fastened it back before dusting off her hands and looking aimlessly around the small cabin. Maybe he hadn't unpacked yet, and in any case, she couldn't very well ask him.

She sat heavily on her bunk and wished whole-heartedly that she could back out of her impulsive agreement to sail with Preston. She pulled out her pillow and fluffed it up and lay back on the still made bunk, fully clothed. She closed her eyes and was soon sound asleep.

Preston quietly opened the door to the cabin, and slipped down the three narrow, wooden steps. The single light bulb was still burning, and he could make out Lacey, fully clothed, sleeping on top of her bunk. He slid out of his jeans and set his watch to beep at four o'clock. His head hit the wall with a resounding thump when he tried to squirm down under the damp sheets. He caught his breath and looked over at Lacey, who only snorted and flipped her arm over her head. He grinned. He could probably do the dishes, or even change her sheets without waking her up. He closed his eyes and fervently hoped Henry wouldn't forget to deliver the goods.

It took Preston a full minute after turning off his watch alarm to remember where he was. Lacey had barely moved since he last looked at her. He watched her chest gently rise and fall to the rhythm of the soft breaths emitting from her nose. He pulled himself out of the sheets, the musty smell lingering on his T-shirt, and tiptoed over to Lacey's bunk and looked down, before guiltily looking away and going into the head. When he came back, he pulled on his jeans and hurried out on deck, but to his dismay, there was no box of supplies awaiting him. He dug in his pocket for change and sprinted up the pier to the pay phone. Henry answered on the tenth ring.

"What happened?"

Henry's voice was raspy with sleep. "Oh, geez, Pres! I fell asleep. What time is it?" he croaked.

"It's ten after four. Hurry. I'll never live it down if we sail without toilet paper."

"I'll be there as soon as I can." Preston hung up and stood a minute before heading determinedly towards the public restrooms. He walked into the men's room, and managed to find two half-rolls of toilet paper, but no soap. He looked furtively around before diving into the women's restroom. Here he had much better luck, finding three full rolls, an unopened package of paper towels, and a full dispenser of liquid soap. He felt no compunction at all about yanking the entire dispenser from the wall and tucking it under his shirt. He sprinted back to the boat and quietly placed his booty in the head.

He tiptoed past Lacey's sleeping form and began checking the fittings on the sails. He wanted the mainsail to unfurl quickly and with little effort. He heard, rather than saw, signs of activity on the other boats, all of which were docked together on one side of the pier. He checked all the lines, the auxiliary batteries, the emergency dinghy, and took a long, hard look at the official race navigational chart.

He figured it should take about five and a half days

to get to Bermuda, and the same coming back. They had to dock at the Mangrove Bay Wharf for forty-eight hours, and pick up supplies. There the racing committee would board the boat again and make sure the auxiliary engine hadn't been used, and that there were the same two crew members on board who had left the dock in Palm Beach. He looked up the pier for Henry. At least he had thought of the public restrooms, but he could just imagine what Lacey would say when she discovered where he had 'shopped.'

Lacey stretched lazily on the bunk and shivered in the cool morning air. Preston was gone, but his bunk looked slept in, so she assumed he had been there at least sometime during the night. She looked around and spotted the dirty dishes right where she had left them. She sighed and went into the bathroom and hastily brushed her teeth.

To her surprise she found rolls of toilet paper, paper towels, and a soap dispenser that looked as if it had been ripped off of a wall. She stored everything under the bathroom sink, though she had to wrestle the liquid soap container out of the dispenser. Happy to finally have some soap at her disposal, she poured some in the kitchen sink, rinsed out a questionably clean saucepan, and started some water boiling on the stove while restacking the dishes neatly on the counter.

She wondered briefly where Preston's dirty plate from last night was, when he frightened her by yelling down into the cabin, "Are you up yet? The yacht club racing judges are inspecting all the boats and they'll be here soon."

"I'm up." She walked towards the door and looked up at him. "Where are your dishes from last night?"

He murmured something, but returned with his dishes in hand before she could reach the doorway. He thrust them towards her. "Here. Can you fix us some coffee or something? We'll be setting sail in less than an hour."

Geez, he was demanding—not even a please or thank-you. "I was going to, as soon as I cleaned up the kitchen you were going to clean last night. I *am* in charge of the kitchen, aren't I?"

"Galley," he said automatically.

She spun around impatiently and poured some of the steaming water in the sink and began scrubbing the frying pan furiously with the worn sponge.

Galley. Lalley. What difference did it make? She had a feeling that he only corrected her to show some sort of superiority, since she had put him so often at a disadvantage since they met. She couldn't help that she was one of those practical, think-ahead people, while he was a useless scatterbrain. Someone had to think of the details, and it was obvious that his only concern was winning this race.

Preston watched as the three judges jumped off the neighboring boat. He fiddled nervously with his shirt tail as they came towards him, and wondered for the umpteenth time where in the hell Henry was.

"Good morning, Rockwell." The taller man stuck out his hand. "Surprised to hear you're racing this year, especially in Reese's boat." He stepped carefully on board after vigorously shaking Preston's hand, and helped the plump female behind him down onto the deck. "You know Louise Gladstone and Harvey Littleton, of course. Is your crew on board?"

Preston cleared his throat. "She's below."

"Your father would have been proud of you, boy, racing after all that's happened. It's something he would have done." The man looked slowly around the deck, before looking Preston straight in the eye. "Quite a gamble you're taking, isn't it?"

"No. A gamble is when you leave it to luck to win. I'm relying on hard work and skill."

"Ah, skill. Are you sure you have enough skill to sail to Bermuda and back?"

"Yes, sir. Don't lose any sleep over my sailing abil-ity."

Murphy grunted and followed the other two judges down into the cabin. Preston clenched his teeth, hop-ing Lacey wouldn't talk too much, and remained de-terminedly on deck, searching the pier for Henry and the supplies.

Lacey turned to see the three judges staring curi-ously at her from the doorway to the cabin. She self-consciously brushed the long tendrils of hair that had escaped from her braid during the night away from her face and wiped her hands on her jeans.

The taller man looked at a piece of paper and then back at Lacey. "Lacey Campbell?" he asked.

"Yes," she answered nervously. These must be the judges.

"Have you known Rockwell long?" The taller man looked her up and down.

"Why? Does it matter?" she asked defensively. "Did I break a rule or something?"

"No." All three looked at each other.

"How experienced a sailor are you?" asked the woman.

"Experienced enough to satisfy Preston, and he's

the one who really counts." She nervously wiped her hands on her jeans again.

"Good luck in the race," the taller man said, his tone of voice indicating he thought she'd need it.

"Scuttle-butt," she mumbled under her breath.

Lacey watched them leave the cabin. They probably thought she was some bimbo Preston had picked up at the last minute. She threw down the sponge, picked up the steaming mug of coffee she had fixed for Preston just as the judges had entered the cabin, and stalked up on deck. They were stepping down to the dock, with Preston stiffly watching them leave. The tension in his body was unmistakable. She walked up beside him, circled his waist with her arm, and handed him the mug of coffee.

"Preston, honey, when do we set sail? I'm finished in the galley." She could see the judges looking at them out of the corner of her eye.

Preston looked startled, but deftly took the coffee. Then he noticed her imperceptibly jerk her head towards the judges. As understanding dawned on him, he impishly put his arm around her shoulders and pulled her closer. "Thanks, Lace." Some impulse, devilish or otherwise, he wasn't sure, made him look down and gently kiss her on the tip of her nose.

This time she was the one who was startled. She stared at him and blushed, before looking over to see the judges walking down the pier towards their boat, their job apparently completed. She pushed away, almost causing Preston to drop his mug.

"What was that for?" she demanded.

He took a casual sip of coffee and almost spit it out. "In the future, I'd like sugar in my coffee. What made you feel they needed that touching little charade?"

Lacey's face went beet red. "I don't know. They acted like I was some kind of vermin or something, and I wanted them to think I've known you for awhile."

"It doesn't matter what they think."

"Not to you, but it does to me. I don't want people thinking you just picked me up in a bar somewhere."

"But I did." Preston suppressed a smile.

"Yeah, but not the way they think. And you didn't have to kiss me." She took his mug from him and walked back into the cabin, her back ramrod straight.

"It was just your nose, for God's sake," he muttered under his breath. He shook his head and began untying all the lines holding the boat to the pier except for the bow line. The boat drifted straight out from the dock and Preston unfurled the mainsail. The wind caught, and the line holding the boat to the dock lifted out of the water. There wasn't much time left before the gun would sound for the race to start. Henry should have been here by now, but he couldn't afford to wait much longer.

"Lacey! I need you on deck!" Preston stood at the wheel and turned the rudder port.

"What?" She was standing with the dish sponge in her hand.

"Go up and untie the bow line."

"The what?"

Preston sighed. "Come here and hold this wheel steady."

She came reluctantly towards him and took hold of the wheel.

"Now don't turn it, not even an inch, and don't let go." He stood back. "Got it?"

"Yes, sir!" She gave a mock salute. "I think I can handle it."

"Keep both hands on the wheel," he snapped before bounding forward and frantically untying the line. The boat began drifting out backwards from the marina. Preston ran back and wrenched the wheel from Lacey's death grip. "You can let go now."

"Do you need me for anything else?"

"Yes, you'll have to swing the boom around as soon as we are parallel to the dock."

"The what?"

"Never mind." He turned the wheel to straighten the rudder and looked impatiently at her. "Hold this again, and don't turn it."

He ran over and started checking the rope that pulled the long pole at the bottom of the sail across the boat. The mainsail swung slowly around and furled out with a snap. The boat began to go rapidly forward, with Preston almost breaking his neck to race back to the wheel.

He pushed her aside unceremoniously, while turning the rudder away from the marina. The boat rapidly glided out to sea to join the other boats bobbing offshore. Preston glanced over at Lacey. She hadn't moved from where he had roughly shoved her. In fact, she was staring raptly at the pier.

"Are you okay?"

She looked at him. "Yes, but something is wrong with your friend, Henry."

Preston looked back at the pier to see Henry waving his arms, and jumping up and down.

"What's he doing? He looks upset."

Before Preston could comment, a cloud of smoke came from a large schooner on the edge of the crowd, followed by a loud boom.

"What was that?" asked Lacey.

"The starting gun. Hold the wheel steady."

Lacey grabbed the wheel and Preston ran over to unfurl a smaller sail in the back of the boat. It too snapped tight and soon they were cutting through the water in a frantic attempt to catch up to the other boats, all thoughts of Henry gone. Lacey gasped as spray shot up in her face.

Preston took the wheel again and grimly guided the boat towards the pack. "Damn."

"What?"

"We're behind before we even got started."

Forty minutes later, Lacey emerged from below in an eye-popping one-piece bathing suit in a blindingly bright, electric blue and some very dark sunglasses. In her hands was his cup of coffee and a small bag. She unself-consciously handed him the coffee without a word and went towards the front of the boat. He idly sipped his coffee, this time with way too much sugar, and tried not to stare at her as she laid out a none too clean beach towel on the deck, and began to lather herself with suntan lotion.

She was acting like they were on a cruise, for God's sake! "What are you doing?" he yelled down at her.

"I'm entertaining myself." She didn't even look up as she put the top back on the lotion and settled on her stomach with a book open in front of her.

"Need I remind you we are in a race?"

Lacey turned and looked haughtily over her sunglasses at him.

"And what do you want me to do, Mr. Rockwell?

Paddle with my hands? Blow into the sails? Stay below to help our wind resistance?"

Smart aleck. She had an answer for everything. "No," he conceded roughly.

"Do you want me to hold the wheel? Fix you a meal? What did you have in mind?"

"Nothing."

"May I return to my book now?"

"Yes." He tore his eyes away from her and concentrated on sailing the boat. The wind was hard and fast, and they had already passed two of the boats. Henry's boat was a sleek ketch built specifically for racing. He checked the barometer to find it was holding steady. He sighed as he finished his coffee, and his eyes strayed down to Lacey's perfect little behind shining in the sun. She had put on so much suntan lotion, he half expected her to slide off the deck and into the ocean. He squinted back into the horizon, wishing he had thought to bring sunglasses like Lacey.

A while later, Preston took the binoculars to look down at the book she was reading. He chuckled at the title. *First Rate, First Mate—Sailing for Beginners*—as if anyone could learn to sail from a book. He had to admire her for trying, though. He trained the binoculars on the horizon. Only two ships were still in sight, but they were too far away to read their names, even with the binoculars. He hadn't seen Rodney and Cynthia since early in the morning as their boat left the marina to rendezvous at the starting line.

Lacey concentrated on her book. She was determined to refresh her basic knowledge and learn everything possible about sailing before evening. No way was Preston Rockwell going to be able to blame her for not winning the race. So far everything was fine. The boat seemed to glide smoothly through the water. Even in the kitchen, she could barely tell they had left the dock.

This might even have been fun, if things were different. If Preston wasn't such a killjoy. If she still had a job. If Frank had married her instead of Jodi and this was her honeymoon.

Four

Lacey sat up and stretched. It was hot on deck, despite the slight spray from the ocean and the steady wind. She stood up and headed for the cabin, stepping carefully over various lines. Halfway there, she looked up to see Preston sitting in a deck chair next to the wheel, which was now secured by a heavy length of rope, staring at her.

"What?" she asked, looking down quickly, hoping her bathing suit hadn't maneuvered off of a vital body part.

"Nothing." He shifted his gaze back to the horizon. So far the trip had been too good to be true. From what he could tell, they were only three boats behind, with the wind still at their back, and steady. He had been able to quit gripping the wheel hours earlier by lashing it firmly to a ring embedded in the deck. He had long ago removed his shirt and was sweating profusely. He wished they could stop long enough so he could take a swim or at least change into some shorts.

"Well, are you hungry yet?" Lacey asked. "I'm going to fix myself something to eat, and I kept your sandwich from this morning."

Preston said no to the sandwich, but he asked for a drink politely enough.

When Lacey got below, she removed the rubber band that was holding her ponytail and brushed her hair vigorously away from her face again. Her natural curl was fighting the restraint of the rubber band because of the humidity, and tendrils of hair kept stubbornly escaping to fly in her face. After fixing her hair, she went over to the ice chest and removed Preston's sandwich from earlier and ate it with gusto.

She was licking her fingers, when she remembered he had asked for a drink. She ran up on deck with a ginger ale and had to bite her tongue when she got close to him, not wanting to admonish him for not eating, or for letting his skin be broiled by the sun. His face was already red, even through the tan, but she was absolutely determined not to say a word.

Preston took the drink from her, wondering what she was thinking and why she was looking at him so intently. After several gulps, he looked into her clear green eyes and asked, "Why are you staring at me?"

She shook her head. "You don't want to know, believe me."

"Why?"

"It's much too motherly for you to handle, but I'll venture to guess that by tomorrow morning, you'll know what I wanted to say right now."

"Well, unless it involves how we can win the race . . ." His voice trailed off as he stood up and untied the wheel, turned it ever so slightly, tied it up again, and sat down.

"Are you planning to sail the boat there and back by yourself?"

Preston looked up at her. "Do I have a choice?"

"Yes. You could tell me what to do so I can relieve you and you can get some rest."

"I'll rest just like I'm resting now."

"So you don't intend to tell me what to do?"

Preston shook his head.

"Eventually, Mr. Rockwell, you'll have to go to the bathroom like everybody else. Or worse, you could get sick or hurt, and I'll have to sail the boat, but since you're in charge, I'll leave the decision-making entirely up to you." She spun around and marched back to her beach towel.

Preston Rockwell was a stubborn nincompoop. She'd just have to learn to sail on her own. She put her sunglasses back on and picked up the how-to-sail book and began poring over the illustration which named the parts of the boat.

Preston remained seated and finished off his drink, wishing she hadn't mentioned him having to go to the bathroom. He shifted in his chair and wondered if he'd be able to run downstairs to and get back before she noticed.

He sat suffering in silence for another twenty minutes before he called down to her. "Can you come up here for a few minutes?" He hated asking her for anything.

She promptly put down her book and walked carefully towards Preston. He couldn't tell what she was thinking behind the dark glasses. She stood silently before him.

"We're, ah, heading northeast, and all you have to do is sit here and make sure the rudder doesn't move, because we're right on course."

"Are you asking me to watch things while you go below?"

"Yes!" he snapped. "Can you handle this?"

"Aye-aye, sir." She sat in his newly vacated deck chair and stared raptly into the compass.

Preston hesitated, half expecting a retort of some kind, before finally turning and disappearing hurriedly down into the cabin. He raced towards the head and marveled at how clean it was. She had obviously put the soap to good use. When he reentered the cabin from the head, he pulled open the storage locker under his bunk and froze. It was empty, and he suddenly realized what he had done. He had set sail with only the clothes on his back. What would she have to say about this?

He sat back on his heels and thought it out. He could sweat profusely in these expensive hot jeans, or cut them off and make shorts. He chose the latter, and hurriedly cut most of the leg material away with a pair of scissors he found in the galley. He threw the material into his locker and hurried back onto deck. Lacey was standing at the wheel, her sunglasses pulled back on her head like a headband, watching the compass the way most people watched television. She didn't look up until he was right next to her.

"This is so easy!" she exclaimed, her eyes shining.

"Yeah, but it's usually not this easy. So far we've been lucky." He took a minute to drink in her excitement. He had never seen anyone this enthralled over something so, well, ordinary. Most of the women he knew were pretty blasé about things. "You can return to your book now."

She stepped away from the wheel and glanced down at his shorts. "You cut off your jeans!"

"Yeah." Lacey looked at him in silence, and he offered no explanation. He could see her mind clicking along and when she finally lifted her eyes to his face, he knew she had figured out that he hadn't remembered to pack for this trip. He wasn't sure what she was thinking, but he had to admire her for merely turning slowly around and going back to her towel.

Preston laid out the charts Henry had gotten for him the day before. They would be staying within sight of the Florida and Georgia coast through the night, but after tomorrow, they would be veering away from land and towards the open sea. He flipped on the Coast Guard weather station. Usually the summers brought violent thunderstorms during the evenings, but so far he didn't even see a stray cloud, and the forecast was just as positive.

His back ached from poring over the charts and sitting stiffly at the wheel. He wished now that he had let Lacey relieve him while the going was smooth. She was right. She should know what to do.

Just as he was about to yell down to her, she startled him by yelling up, "Preston?"

"What?"

"Don't we have a tarp or something to set up over the wheel?"

Preston looked puzzled. His boat had had an enclosed pilot house, but he had assumed Henry's was meant to be open-air. A tarp hadn't occurred to him, but then, that wasn't a surprise. Lacey had set down her book and removed the glasses, and was making her way towards him.

"It says here that we should have some kind of weather tarp over the wheel to keep the glare down and protect the captain. That's you," she added. She squinted up behind him and pointed. "Is that blue stuff used for anything that has to do with sailing?"

Preston looked up. "No . . . I guess it's probably the tarp." He reached up and loosened the ropes that lashed the heavy blue plastic sheet together. He hadn't even noticed it before. Lacey reached up and took one side and they pulled it straight out and hooked it to a slender metal frame which was already in place. She looked at him and smiled.

"See—we can work together as a team. Isn't that better?"

Preston couldn't answer. Lacey's face was slightly red from the sun and the exertion, and it made her eyes take on an unnaturally brilliant green color. And when she had just smiled at him, he was suddenly dazzled. She was very beautiful, and in the skin-tight electric blue bathing suit showing her every curve, he was having a very hard time trying not to think of her as a female.

He cleared his throat. "Yes. Thank you." His body was beginning to react to her closeness, and he nervously turned and headed back to the wheel. "By the way, you were right. You should learn to sail—just in case. Come here and I'll show you what you need to know."

Her smile grew even wider, showing two distinct dimples in her cheeks he had never before noticed. Well, actually, before today, he had never really seen her smile. She hurried to his side and listened intently as he gave a quick lesson on reading the charts, watching the compass and barometer, working the radio, and turning the wheel. Her questions were sharp and clever, but for once he didn't feel intimidated. In a little over a hour, he felt fairly confident that she could sail the boat while he rested, as long as they weren't in any kind of bad weather.

"Don't get mad," Lacey began, "but I think we should take shifts at sailing so that neither of us gets too tired." She waited nervously for his reaction.

Preston rubbed the back of his neck with one of his hands as he looked off into the horizon. Finally he looked back at her. "You're right again. If we are going to win this thing, we are going to have to work together, and I obviously can't do it on my own." He grinned suddenly, surprising her. "Besides, so far you've been a big help, and you know that I hate to admit it."

Lacey laughed. "Thank you, Captain. I aim to please, and remember, I want to win this race as much as you do!"

Preston felt weeks of tension leave his body at her laugh. This is what he desperately needed. Fun, a chance to laugh, a chance to forget his financial woes. He smiled.

"Since things seem to be going rather smoothly right now, I think I'll go down and take a quick nap. Then I can sail the night shift, and you can sail the days, weather permitting."

Lacey's smile left her face. "You mean we sail at night, too?"

"It is a race, you know. Boats don't stop moving at night. They don't need to rest," he grinned and went below.

Preston emerged just as the sun was setting, looking rumpled and grumpy, his face alarmingly red. Lacey wasn't at her best either, feeling stiff and bored from looking at the endless horizon and staring at the compass. He didn't speak, but stood expectantly by her chair until she got up slowly and stretched. "I didn't touch a thing," she offered.

He squinted at the compass and then reached down for the chart. After a few minutes, he put the chart back and untied the wheel to turn it sharply to the right.

"What? Did I do something wrong?" she asked worriedly.

"No."

She hesitated before asking, "Do you want something to eat?"

"I'm not hungry," he grunted.

She started to say something, but his look quelled her. She felt a disappointment wash over her which she couldn't explain. Earlier, for a few magic minutes, she had thought they might be friends, but somehow, Preston had gotten up on the wrong side of the bunk after his nap.

She went down and began puttering in the galley, as he insisted on calling the tiny area, when she heard him calling her. She ran up the steps, thinking he was going to apologize for being curt, or maybe needed her in some way.

"Get me some coffee," he barked as he cranked the boom to the left.

Lacey stood still and waited, not moving. Her eyes narrowed, and if looks could kill, Preston would have just drawn his last breath.

He looked up at her. "Only one sugar," he added, hoping she'd disappear. Still she stood there.

Preston felt a slow flush build in his face as he realized how rude he probably sounded to her. But the wind had shifted during his nap, and it had taken some fast maneuvering to get the boat back on course. "Please," he added meekly, not wanting her angry at him again.

She turned and slammed into the cabin. She quickly made his coffee and took it up on deck, thrusting it at him without spilling a drop or saying a word.

"Thank you," he called out as she disappeared below. At the stove, she threw together a meal of creamed chipped beef. Soon she was eating with enthusiasm at the small table for two.

Preston sipped on the insipid coffee and sniffed the air appreciatively. Whatever she was cooking up smelled divine, but he was damned if he would ask her for any. He snapped on the running lights, glad Henry had lacquered the bulbs around the outside of the cabin and over the helm red to prevent glare and light blindness. If anything, the wind had picked up, and they were smoothly cutting through the slight swells. He wondered what Lacey would do when they were out in the real ocean where waves could hide them from a boat less than a mile away.

Preston set down his coffee cup and slouched in his chair. He could see a light from the cabin and hear the clinks and clanks from dishes being washed or put away through the open hatch. Soon the sounds stopped and the light went off, and he assumed she had nestled down into her bunk for the night.

Lacey lay staring at the dark ceiling, wondering what on earth happened to the nice, smiling skipper whom she had almost started liking earlier. It must have been an act, or extreme fatigue that made him forget to be ornery, demanding, and nasty for a moment. An oversight on his part, she was sure. She punched her pillow and turned towards the wall of the cabin, and went quickly to sleep, dressed in her clothes from the day before.

Preston kept a steady eye on the compass, almost catching himself nodding off several times. His face and chest were burning ominously. He had never sunburned before, but then he had never sat out in blazing sunshine for an entire day before, either. Suddenly overcome with chills, he hurriedly went down to pull the blanket off his bunk to wrap himself in. He could hear Lacey snoring softly. Delicate, feminine snores, almost like purring. Had she sneaked a cat on board? Maybe he was beginning to hallucinate. He rushed back to his chair and hunkered down for the night, his teeth clattering.

Lacey awoke to the sounds of whales mating. Or was it harbor seals fighting? Her eyes flew open and she listened more closely. She was hearing groans: low, pain-wracked, animal groans. She jumped off her bunk and hurried onto deck to find Preston slumped in his chair, his face in shades of pale green to fiery red, wrapped in a blanket, shaking uncontrollably, and making the most awful noises.

"Oh my gosh! What's wrong? Are you seasick? What happened?"

She ran over and helped him up to lead him carefully below to his berth.

"Sun poisoning, I think," he whispered, his legs quaking with the effort it took to move himself, even with Lacey there to lean on.

She resisted saying 'I told you so,' and thrust him unceremoniously onto his bunk, yanking her own bedding off and spreading it sloppily over him. "When you're up to it, rub yourself in this lotion, and take some aspirin." She threw two bottles onto the bunk next to him and left the cabin.

What was she to do? She was only on chapter six of the sailing book! She wasn't sure if Preston had them on the correct course, or if he had become sick early in the night and they were headed nowhere. She pulled at the charts and frantically checked them, but threw them down immediately. She had no idea of their location, so the charts were virtually useless. The sails were rigid in the wind, and they were moving at an incredible pace. She decided that since Bermuda was to the northeast, she'd just steer in that direction. Turning the rudder would do no good if the sails weren't facing the right way to benefit from the full impact of the wind. After much maneuvering and cranking of the winch controlling the booms of the mainsail and the smaller one in back, she was finally satisfied enough to sit back in her chair and relax for the first time in what seemed like hours, extremely proud of herself

She looked up at the sky and noticed that there were a few clouds blocking the sun, and the waves, which yesterday had been mere swells, were now small hills of water. Still, the boat was sailing smoothly except for an occasional slap the bow made when it met an errant wave.

She reached down and pulled a small book from underneath the charts. It was the ship's log for—she looked closely, not quite believing her eyes—the *Stud Muffin*. The *Stud Muffin*? She was sailing to Bermuda on a boat named the *Stud Muffin*? For the first time in many months, she began to laugh. She laughed so hard, her sides hurt, for no one ever looked less like a stud muffin than Preston Rockwell did right now.

Wiping tears of laughter from her eyes, she made sure the wheel was lashed firmly in place, and, still chuckling, she tiptoed into the cabin to find Preston huddled in the blankets. He hadn't opened the lotion or the aspirin. In fact, he hadn't moved. He looked terrible.

"Sit up!" Lacey said firmly. She fetched a cup of water and forced open his mouth and made him swallow some aspirin. She noticed his eyes were almost swollen shut, his skin was hot and feverish, and large blisters were already beginning to form on his face.

"You have to get up," she said, worried.

"Quit torturing me." His voice was weak and muffled in the bedclothes he had already pulled back over his face.

She grabbed the covers and pulled them off the bed. "Cooperate or I'll get ugly."

"What do you want?" Preston's eyes were mere angry slits.

"I want to get these clothes off you and get some of this lotion onto your skin. There are serious burns on your face, so I can only imagine what your back, chest, and legs look like."

"I'm not undressing in front of you." He made a feeble attempt to take back at least the sheets.

She grabbed his arms, wincing at his groan of pain. "Preston, listen to me. I need you to help me sail this boat. Do you still want to win this race?"

He suddenly quit struggling. "I've got to win." He sounded so pathetic, so forlorn, that she instantly forgave him every stupid thing he had done so far.

"I know, Preston. But you can't do it in this condition, and I can't do it alone." She gently pushed his damp hair off his face with her fingers. "You have to protect your skin from the sun because I'm going to need you back on deck eventually. So just let me take care of you, okay?"

He hung his head sheepishly. "Okay, but don't look while I undress."

She stifled a smile and turned her back, resisting the urge to help him when she heard him struggling frantically with his shorts.

"You can look now."

Lacey turned and grimaced at the condition of his face, where a few blisters were beginning to ooze. "Now I'm going to rub this lotion on you, and I promise it will make you feel better."

"I'll do it myself." He grabbed for the bottle.

"No." She pushed him back on the bed. "You'll lay here and behave so I can get outside and make sure everything is okay."

That stopped him and he lay quietly with his eyes closed and let her peel back the sheets to his waist. She squirted some of the lotion in her hands and warmed it between her palms before gently rubbing it onto his burning skin. Some of the blisters were sizeable, and she carefully avoided popping them. Preston gave a shuddering sigh. Whether it was in pain, in resignation, or in ecstasy, she wasn't quite sure, but he had totally quit resisting her.

"Are you a nurse or something?" he asked.

She smiled. "No. I'm a redhead."

He opened his eyes as far as he could and frowned. "I noticed. Guess you could write a book on sunburn care."

"Well, I've been in the same fix you're in right now

more times than I can remember. I finally gave up trying to tan, or in my case, trying to run my freckles together to look like a tan, and now I slather on lots of sunblock lotion instead."

"And to think I laughed at you." He closed his eyes again.

She stopped rubbing. "You did? When?"

"When you plastered yourself with lotion yesterday while you were sunbathing on deck."

"I didn't think you noticed me do anything yesterday."

"Oh, I noticed." He stopped.

She began rubbing the lotion on his arms, a frown furrowing her brow. She could have sworn that all he had noticed yesterday had been her ineptness at sailing, and the wind speed and direction. Somehow it intrigued her that he had watched her sunbathe.

"Turn over, I'll do your back."

Preston seemed more than willing to comply now.

Lacey slowly and methodically rubbed lotion on his back, surprised at how solid and hard his muscles were. He didn't look muscular, or if he did, she hadn't noticed before. His back, like his chest, was lacking the bushy, curly, dark hair she had once admired on Frank. Instead he had soft, golden threads of hair growing in what seemed to be just the right places. She covered him back up to the neck, and lifted the sheets from his legs to just below the soft swells of his buttocks. She took a deep breath, and began rubbing his legs, which, fortunately for him, weren't as red as his chest and back.

"Turn over." Lacey's voice was hoarse, and she was surprised that he heard, and obeyed her. She began rubbing the front of his thighs, her eyes straying repeatedly to the fascinating mound where his legs met. He groaned, and Lacey flushed as she saw the unmistakable signs of his arousal beneath the sheets. She hurriedly pulled them back over his legs and put the bottle in Preston's hand.

"You do your face. I've got to see how we're doing out there," she rasped as she scurried from the cabin. Lacey wiped her brow with her sleeve. What was wrong with her? She distractedly checked the compass, even though she knew distraction could be dangerous. Preston Rockwell, in the matter of a split second, had suddenly become a threat to her. She was vulnerable. He was no longer a racing partner with a bad attitude. He was something far more dangerous. An attractive man. A virile man.

She felt her face flush again. *Snap out of it, Lacey. Men are poison. He'll hurt you, just like your father did. Just like Frank did.* But as she sat there, staring into the horizon, she could only see the look of absolute adoration and love Frank had given Jodi the last time she saw them together, and the looks of pride and love Tom gave her mother all the time, and in a tiny, hidden core of herself, she knew all too well that she wanted someone to look at her like that one day.

Five

When Preston finally emerged from the cabin, the sun was just beginning to lower itself into the western horizon. Lacey watched him wobble painfully up behind her chair, and felt herself go rigid as he looked over her shoulder at the compass. She could feel the heat from his sunburn through her thin cotton shirt.

He consulted the charts, checked the compass, and looked carefully at the sails, before gingerly going around the deck and checking all the rigging. Lacey nervously fingered the strands of red hair which had come loose from her ponytail and had fallen over her forehead. He finally returned and looked at her in wonder. "Are you sure you've never sailed in a race before?"

She felt a rush of elation at the admiring tone of his voice. "Never." She brushed the errant tendrils from her face with her fingers and smiled.

"We're right on course, and we're moving at optimum speed. You did a great job while I was goofing off all day," he said derisively.

She looked sharply at him, the smile leaving her face. "You were hardly goofing off. You were sick from too much sun and not enough food." Her eyes widened and she clapped her hand over her mouth. She hadn't meant to bring that up again.

Instead of looking angry, Preston gave a weak smile. "I know. I apologize for not letting you take care of me."

Lacey flushed with pleasure. He was standing so close she could smell the sweet scent of the lotion she had smoothed on his skin earlier, which brought to mind images of him stretched out on his bunk, and she felt her face grow even warmer. "That's okay," she said softly, looking away. "I think we've both been under some stress lately."

Preston sighed. "That's an understatement. You go on below and rest. I'll take over." She got up and let him sit in the chair.

"Are you sure you feel up to it?" She stood looking down at him. He still didn't look well to her and she could tell the chair was uncomfortable against his sunburn.

He reached for the binoculars and carefully placed them next to his face. "I'm fine."

When Lacey reached the inside of the cabin, she decided to make Preston and herself a hearty meal, before she got some much needed rest. She took Preston up a can of ginger ale while the food was heating, but he shook his head.

"Please drink it. Severe sunburn makes you dehydrated."

Preston grunted and took the can ungraciously, frowning at the horizon. "Did you see any other boats today at all?"

"I thought I did earlier, but I wasn't sure."

"I can't figure out why we haven't seen anyone." He bent his head back towards the charts.

"I'm bringing you something to eat in a minute."

"Lacey, my stomach is in knots. I'm not hungry."

"But, Preston—"

He held up his hands in mock surrender. "Never mind. I know what you're going to say. I'll eat, but I'm not hungry."

Lacey hurried back to the galley and prepared him a plate. Something had changed between her and Preston, and she wasn't sure at all that she liked the course they were on.

Preston took a deep breath and sat back slowly in his chair. He had eaten so fast, he had hardly tasted the food. He guessed he had been hungry after all. Well, more like starving. He was glad Lacey had made him eat. He had watched her nervously hand him his plate and avoid eye contact with him all evening. Even though he realized the running lights were casting eerie shadows on her face, he didn't think it was the lighting which was causing her to look so drawn and almost frightened. When she came over to take his dishes, his hand grazed hers and she jumped, dropping his empty mug and breaking it.

"Oh!" She bent down and frantically began picking up the pieces as if someone were about to punish her.

"What's wrong with you?" Preston demanded, squatting next to her.

"I'm fine." She stood up and hurried down into the cabin, leaving a few pieces of broken china on the deck. He picked them up and tossed them overboard.

He shook his head. She was certainly acting strange. He almost liked the bitchy Lacey better. At least he understood her.

Lacey leaned against the galley sink, and slowly lowered her chin onto her chest. What on earth was wrong with her? She was acting like a fool. She only knew she definitely liked the cold, impersonal, arrogant Preston better. That Preston, she could deal with.

Unable to bear the same clothes another minute, Lacey kicked off her sneakers and changed into a yellow tank top and a pair of navy shorts. She padded to the head and brushed her teeth. It took her several minutes to brush the tangles from the hair that had escaped from the rubber band during her long day of duty on deck. Once she had removed the tangles, she walked back to her bunk, rebraiding her hair. After retrieving her blanket from Preston's bed, she curled up on the bare mattress, and fell soundly asleep.

Lacey slept much later than she had wanted. Luckily for her, the gentle bouncing of the boat was soothing, almost comforting, rather than nauseating as she had feared. She leapt out of bed and raced onto deck to find Preston exactly where she had left him.

She went up and gingerly touched his shoulder. "Preston?"

His head snapped up and he looked blankly around until his eyes focused on her. "What?"

"You can go below, now." She helped him out of the chair. Suddenly his legs buckled, and he leaned heavily against her. Lacey attempted to hold him up, but couldn't withstand his full weight. They fell together, almost in slow motion, and landed in a heap, with Lacey firmly pressed against the deck by Preston's full length.

He looked down into her flushed face. "I'm sorry. I lost my balance. Are you hurt?" He felt amazingly comfortable where he was, and made no effort to get up.

"No, I'm fine. I should have supported you better." Her eyes focused on the beginnings of a golden beard on his face, which was mere inches from her own. She didn't struggle to get up, either.

She lifted her green eyes to his brown ones and felt their breathing suddenly harmonize for a full twenty seconds before they both simultaneously struggled to stand upright, as if afraid of what they saw. Studiously avoiding looking at him again, Lacey helped him below with as little actual physical contact as possible. Preston lay down in his bunk, without arguing, for a wonder. She hurried back on deck, glad to be out of his disturbing presence.

At first Lacey had been startled, and then enthralled, by the school of porpoises that appeared from nowhere to escort the boat. It was another perfect day for sailing. The wind was still strong and steady at their back, and at times the *Stud Muffin* seemed to barely skim the surface of the ocean. Lacey had to check the compass only occasionally, and after two hours of little required effort, she finally allowed herself to relax.

She had put her bathing suit back on earlier because it was less constrictive than her shorts, and it was hot sitting under the tarp. She also lathered herself in sunblock lotion, knowing the glare could be as lethal as the sun's direct rays. She had spotted another boat on the horizon earlier, but peer as she might, she could not make out the name of the craft. She looked up the flag which was flying from the other boat's mast in her book, and determined it was definitely one of the competition.

Around noon, she listened at the hatch for any motion from inside the cabin, but heard nothing from Preston. At one, her stomach demanded food, so she secured everything on deck, and went below to concoct something to eat.

To her surprise, Preston's eyes were open, and he was stretched out comfortably with his arms under his head. He raised himself on one elbow. "Do you need me?"

"No, ah—I'm just hungry." Lacey departed hastily for the galley and Preston lay back down, uncertain whether he felt relieved or disappointed.

"Do you want me to fix you something? I'd better use these eggs while they're fresh. How about another omelet?" She looked over her shoulder at him, her escaped hair flying about her face.

"That would be perfect." He watched, fascinated, as Lacey cracked eggs into a bowl, emptying the shells while still holding them in one hand like a professional chef. She moved with ease and poise about the tiny galley, despite the jerky movements of the boat. She had changed into the revealing blue bathing suit again, and his eyes kept straying from her competent hands, to the generous swells of her breasts straining against the thin, stretchy material. She glanced up to see him staring at her, and they both guiltily looked away.

In minutes she had made a fluffy ham omelet, using the last of the eggs, and some canned ham. She brought his plate to him as he scooted up to sit upright on his bunk.

"Looks good," he said, digging in. Lacey put her

omelet between two slices of bread and took a huge bite. Sailing made her hungry. They ate in silence, and when he was finished, she took his plate from him and put it in the sink. "I'll do these later. I better get back on deck."

She started for the cabin door and suddenly stopped as she remembered something. "Oh yeah, I think I can see one of our competitors ahead of us."

Preston started to slide off the bunk. Lacey put both hands on his shoulders and pushed him back down. "Where do you think you're going?"

"To check."

"Look, it has the same bright yellow burgee as we do, but not even you could tell whose boat it is."

"What did you say?"

"I said, you won't—"

"No, the 'B' word."

"What?" she looked puzzled.

"Burgee. How do you know the word burgee?"

Her face turned red. "It's no big deal, Preston. It's the swallow-tailed yacht club flag at the top of our mast and all our competitors have one."

Preston leaned back on his pillow. "I'll take your word for it. Wake me up around five."

Lacey saluted. "Aye-aye!"

"Please," he added to her back.

Lacey didn't wake Preston at five, or for that matter, six. She was having a wonderful time, and he needed the rest far more than she did. The wind had died a little, and they were definitely moving slower than they had been. But somehow the *Stud Muffin* was managing to gain on the boat ahead of them.

When Preston finally emerged from below, it was almost eight, and the sun had become a brilliant orange ball setting in the west. He looked much better, but his skin was starting to peel in earnest, and he was itching terribly.

"Want me to put on a different lotion to stop the itching?" she offered.

He glared at her in silence. Lacey finally got up and walked demurely into the cabin, soundly slamming the door behind her.

Lacey wondered if Preston was aware of the three days' worth of stubble on his face, or that his perfectly cut hair was sticking out wildly everywhere. She grinned. He didn't seem so high and mighty now that he was grubby. And speaking of grubby, she was beginning to feel that way herself. The steady sea spray, not to mention all the lotion she had slathered on in the last few days, made her feel sticky and dirty. She was long overdue for a good scrubbing, and Preston would be occupied enough for her to heat some water and take what her mother had called a bird-bath.

Her frizzled hair was getting on her nerves, and on a sudden impulse, while the water heated on the burner, she cut off her long red locks within a few inches of her scalp with a rusty pair of scissors she had found after rummaging through all the drawers. She wished she had a mirror to look in so she could even things up, but it didn't really matter. She knew only that she was heartily sick of having her hair flying in her face.

When the water on the stove was hot, she took the bottle of soap and squirted it into the saucepan. She searched until she found the leg material of Preston's jeans in his still empty locker, and cut a square out for herself to use as a washcloth. She hurriedly undressed and began scrubbing herself vigorously.

Preston squinted into the darkness at the running lights of the boat just minutes ahead. When he took over his watch, he only had to turn the mainsail and mizzen a fraction to take better advantage of the waves and wind. Lacey had done a great job, but he chided himself for not coming up sooner, for if he had made these two little adjustments three hours ago, they would have already passed the boat ahead and he was certain it was Rodney's boat, the *Filthy Rich*. He could hear his own heart beating in his ears, and felt a rush of adrenaline, wondering if this was the same feeling of excitement that had helped ruin his father. He had to tell Lacey.

"We're passing Rodney and Cynthia . . ." he said as he threw open the cabin door. His voice trailed off as he drank in the sight of Lacey, naked, standing still as a statue, her skin still glimmering with drops of water, shining under the light of the single light bulb. When his eyes finally came back to meet hers, she began a screaming tirade to cover her embarrassment.

"Get out! A gentleman wouldn't stare! You pervert!" She grabbed the blanket from her bed and wrapped it around herself.

"Sorry," Preston mumbled, slamming the door shut. He rushed back to his chair, but somehow the thought of passing Rodney wasn't on his mind as much as the thrill of seeing Lacey Campbell nude.

Lacey paced inside the cabin for a good forty minutes before she finally decided there was no way to avoid future encounters with Preston unless she jumped overboard. She might as well make the best of it and pretend nothing had happened.

Preston was surprised to see Lacey eventually reappear on deck. She even brought him a sandwich and another ginger ale. He took it gratefully and began eating, surprised she chose to join him on deck to eat her own meal. She was still avoiding eye contact, so he thought it best not to mention their earlier encounter. She finally spoke.

"So, we passed Rodney and Cynthia, I see. Are you sure it was them?"

"Oh, it was the *Filthy Rich* all right. They weren't on deck when I sounded the signal for passing, but you should have seen them scramble up after!"

Preston watched her face in the glow of the running lights. "I've never seen Fleming move so fast," he added.

Lacey looked back to see the tiny running lights of the other boat in back of them. "How come we're able to pass them and we're all using the same wind?" she asked curiously.

"Superior sailing ability," he answered smugly. "That and the fact that Henry had this boat built specifically to race. Rodney's is more of a pleasure craft. He's never entered this race before."

"Have you?"

Preston threw his bread crust overboard. "A few times."

"Did you ever win?"

"No," he answered shortly. "But I will this time."

Lacey set her can down with a bang. "I?"

Preston glanced over to see her glowering at him in the semi-darkness.

"I mean we. You've been a great help, Lacey. Much better than I expected."

"Thanks for noticing," she said sarcastically.

"Is there something bothering you?"

"No!" she snapped.

"Are you sure? I mean you've been acting different lately."

"Different than what? You don't even know me."

Preston didn't say anything.

"And talk about different, you have violent mood swings yourself. I never know who's going to greet me—the grumpy Preston or the grateful one."

"I admit I haven't exactly been at my best on this trip, but I really am grateful for all your help."

Lacey remained silent. Minutes ticked by, until Preston could contain himself no longer.

"Why did you cut your hair?"

"It was bugging me."

"It was so long, though."

"It'll grow back."

"Well, I liked it better long."

"Since we are merely sailing partners, I really don't care what you like."

"What did I do to get you so defensive tonight?" he asked, frustrated.

"Nothing. It's just my hair is none of your business."

"Well, at least now I know you're a natural redhead." He knew he shouldn't have said it, but she had snapped his head off one too many times tonight.

"Of all the rude, horrible things to say." She stood up and grabbed for a nearby rope as she almost lost her balance. "I thought just maybe you'd be able to act as if nothing happened earlier, but you just couldn't do it, could you? I knew you'd have to bring it up sometime."

"I'm sorry. I won't mention it again."

"Oh, yes you will. One day, when you are losing an argument, or I get the best of you, you'll bring it up again." She picked up her can and started for the cabin door.

"Lacey, I—"

She held up her hand. "Save it, I'm not up to a full-scale argument tonight." And with that she went below and slammed the cabin door.

Preston sat back in his chair. If she hadn't gotten under his skin somehow, he'd never have mentioned seeing her naked. He wasn't normally so crass, but then his life hadn't been normal in months. Right now something was bothering him about Lacey Campbell, and it bothered him more that he was even thinking of anything else besides the race. There would be plenty of time to think of Lacey, or for that matter, any other female, after he won the money and got his life back in order.

Six

Lacey awoke earlier than usual. Something was wrong, and it took several minutes before she realized that the boat was not moving. Maybe Preston had been swept overboard and she was floundering at sea alone! The thought produced mixed emotions. Deciding to investigate, she ran up on deck and immediately noticed the water surrounding them was still as glass, the sails hanging limp from the masts.

"What's happening?"

"We're in a calm. A dead calm."

"What does that mean?"

"It means we're not moving," he yelled.

"Okay. Excuse me for asking. I meant weather-wise!" she said loudly.

"I can't believe this is happening. I've never seen it like this. Never." He began pacing the deck, ignoring her as if she hadn't spoken. He lifted his binoculars and scanned the horizon.

"If we can't move, no one else can, so relax." Lacey took pity on him.

Preston looked at her and laughed bitterly. "Relax? I can't relax. This could last for days."

"What do you want to do, row? Dive in, grab the back of the boat and paddle? It's out of your control,

Preston. Go down and rest, get something to eat, or maybe shave and wash up."

Preston put his hand self-consciously to his face and felt the four days' worth of stubble. "Well, I guess there's nothing I can do anyway, but swear you'll wake me up as soon as a breeze starts."

"I double, triple swear. Now go brush your teeth or something."

Preston finally went below, leaving a delighted Lacey on deck. She had been dying to take a swim since she first smelled the salty sea air, and it looked like now might be her chance.

She slipped off her shorts and top to reveal her bathing suit and dived eagerly into the clear, cool water. She made no sound as she glided around the boat with strong, easy strokes. She leisurely turned over and floated on her back. It was wonderful out here, and it occurred to her that she hadn't thought of Frank and Jodi for two whole days.

After paddling languidly around the *Stud Muffin* until her fingertips began to wrinkle, she reluctantly pulled herself up and dried herself with one of Henry's stiff towels. She tiptoed down into the cabin and heard Preston's soft, even breathing from the doorway. Her stomach was growling ferociously, so she decided to risk waking him in order to make herself a peanut butter and jelly sandwich. When she reached his side, she couldn't resist looking down at him.

He was even more handsome asleep. Gone were the wrinkles of worry and the perpetual frown that marred his forehead. Asleep, he looked no more than twenty, and for the first time she wondered at his real age. Most of the sunburnt skin had peeled

off his face already, and the new skin was a healthy
pink through the golden stubble. He grunted and
flipped onto his stomach. She hurried into the galley.
He was too good-looking. That was the problem.

Hours later she heard Preston banging pans
around, but resisted the urge to see what he was up
to. When he finally came outside it was late afternoon, and the familiar scent of the liquid soap
floated towards her. Though his stubble remained,
his blonde hair sparkled in the sunlight, and was
neatly combed. He was chomping on a huge sandwich.

"What on earth is that?"

"It's a peanut butter and banana sandwich," he
mumbled.

"Didn't Elvis die from eating those?"

He swallowed. "Then I bet he died happy."

He came over to the chair and looked down at the
barometer, and then scanned the horizon. "Look!"
he pointed excitedly. "Clouds."

"So?"

"So, if they move, there's a wind working up somewhere, and we're bound to get it here eventually."

"Well, you didn't honestly think we were doomed
to sit here forever, did you?"

Preston ignored her, threw his crust overboard,
and put his hands on his hips.

"Why did you do that? It drives me crazy."

He looked at her, frowning. "Do what?"

"Throw your crust away."

"I don't like crust." He looked back towards the
clouds. "I guess because our housekeeper, Florence,
always cut it off my sandwiches when I was growing
up."

"Florence? I thought you had a mother."

"I did, but she didn't cook."

"What did she do?"

Preston shrugged. "I don't know, go to parties and stuff, I think." He didn't like the way her lips were curling. "Why? What did your mother do?"

"She worked at two different jobs to support us after my father left," she answered bitterly. "And we had to eat our crust."

Preston truly didn't know what to say. For the first time in his life, he realized that not everyone was raised the way he was, and not everyone had had it easy. He almost felt guilty until he remembered that he wasn't in much better shape financially right now than Lacey and her mother must have been.

"I'm sorry," he muttered apologetically.

"I don't want your pity, Preston. We did just fine." She got up and started for the cabin. "Do you want dinner or are you full?"

"I'm still starving. I have days of not eating to catch up on." He patted his stomach.

"Okay." She vanished below.

Preston sat down and rested his head on the back of the chair and stared up at the blue tarp. He almost felt sorry for Lacey growing up so poor, yet she was obviously stronger for it, or at least stronger than he. It appeared money had robbed him of common sense, and it was frightening to think that if he didn't win this race, he'd have to somehow support his mother and himself, and certainly not in the style to which they were accustomed.

He had naturally gone to the University of Virginia for his law degree, just as the rest of the men in his family had done for generations, and had passed the

Florida bar exam with ease, but he had never really had to depend on his degree to earn money. He and his father had established a lucrative investment business, guiding clients onto sure ways to make money. He didn't know what it was like to live from paycheck to paycheck, the way so many people did. There was so much he had been protected from, and that Lacey had already faced and conquered.

Lacey opened cans, several of them, and threw the contents together in a saucepan. The combination of pork barbecue, corn, tomatoes, and beans had sounded awful when she first read it in the back of her sailing book, but she was starving, and the way Preston just wolfed down that sandwich, she knew she had better fix a lot. After she stirred the concoction and it simmered awhile, it began to smell heavenly. She made herself some hot tea and Preston some coffee. She took a big bowl of the improvised stew and his coffee up to him. He was looking down into the bowl and wrinkling his nose when she turned to get her dinner from below.

"What is this?" he asked when she got back, pushing it around in his bowl with his spoon.

"Something a rich man's cook would never serve." She started eating with enthusiasm.

Preston watched her for a few minutes before slowly lifting a spoonful and putting it gingerly in his mouth. It didn't take him long after that to empty the bowl. He looked up to see Lacey looking at him with a smug look on her face.

"Was it good?" she asked.

Preston nodded sheepishly. "It was delicious. May I please have some more?" he asked meekly.

Lacey stood and held her hand out for his bowl,

and disappeared downstairs. When she gave him the second helping, he dug in without hesitation. Two bowlfuls later, he finally sat back with a contented sigh and rubbed his stomach.

"Who taught you to cook?"

"My mom. I had to cook my own dinners the nights when she worked as a waitress."

"You must have some mother, Lacey."

"She had to be, to make up for my father," she said, then her voice softened. "I love my mother very much. She deserves everything that's happened to her."

"What's happened to her?" He was curious as to what made Lacey so dreamy-eyed.

"She met a wonderful man two years ago who is very well off. He gives her everything she has ever wanted."

"You mean furs, diamonds, a mansion?"

Lacey gave him a disgusted look. "I mean love, respect, kindness, consideration, friendship, and the opportunity to relax and enjoy life for a change. My mother has earned her right to live in comfort."

Her voice implied that he hadn't, which wounded him for some reason. He didn't answer.

"Money and material things aren't everything to everyone, Preston," she added.

"Why did you agree to sail with me, Lacey? Wasn't it for the money?" he couldn't resist asking.

Lacey had the grace to blush. "Well, yes, but that's different."

"Money is money, and it does the same things for all people." Preston turned and busied himself studying charts, plotting their position, and generally ignoring her, so she took the dirty dishes down below and began cleaning up the galley.

Preston was right. She was here for the money, and it was fairly easy money, at that. No self-respecting woman would have left on a lark like she had. She should have applied for jobs, gone to the YWCA to stay, asked her mother to send her some of her savings. Sometimes, she decided, she had too much pride for her own good. She slammed the saucepan onto the burner to heat up water to do the dishes. But if she hadn't come on this trip, she could have lived her whole life without having an adventure, and she never would have known Preston.

Lacey returned on deck just as the sun was setting. The sky was every shade of pink and gold imaginable. Preston was standing at the back of the boat with his hands on his hips, watching the sunset, a black silhouette on the brilliantly colored background. He emanated strength and determination. She knew if he was capable, he'd summon hurricane force winds to continue them on their way. She slipped up behind him and cleared her throat.

Preston turned around so fast it startled her and she lost her balance. If it hadn't been for his instinctive reaching to catch her, and subsequent grabbing at one of the lines hanging near his head, they would have both plunged overboard.

As it was, Lacey still felt in over her head, for Preston's bare chest was hotly pressed against the thin material of her bathing suit. She could feel the blood rush to her face as they clung together and Preston worked to maintain their balance. He didn't immediately let her go and she wasn't sure she wanted him to. It was comforting to be held in someone's arms.

He looked down at her in the twilight. "You startled me."

She looked down and focused on the golden chest hair near her face. "I'm sorry."

Preston realized that in a moment she might figure out just how pleased he was to hold her so closely, so he gently pushed her away.

Lacey felt like a fool for not pushing herself away sooner. Her heart was pounding, and she couldn't look at him, so she moved to the outer edge of the boat and looked down into the glassy water. Reflections of a million stars sparkled there and she instantly looked up. Relieved to change the subject, she pointed skyward. "Look at all the stars. I've never seen so many at one time."

Preston looked up. "In all the times I've been sailing, I never noticed them before."

Lacey was amazed. "How could you not notice?"

"Well, I was busy with other priorities," he said dryly.

"Such as?" Lacey prodded.

"Women, beer, good times."

"Oh." He could hear the disappointment in her voice. Somehow, he wanted her to know that he had changed.

"I was quite the man-about-town at one time. I'm different now. I've grown up."

"Since when?"

"Since six months ago."

"How old are you, Preston?"

"Thirty-two."

"Isn't thirty-two pretty late in life to grow up?"

"Some people never do."

"What happened six months ago?"

Preston hesitated.

"You don't have to tell me if you don't want to," she offered, trying to mask her hurt.

"I haven't talked about it much to anyone. It's not easy for me." Preston sat down and nervously rubbed the back of his neck with his hand. "Six months ago, my father killed himself."

Lacey had expected that the turn-around for Preston had been when Cynthia had dumped him, not something as serious as his father's suicide. "Oh, Preston, I'm so sorry."

"I'm okay about it now."

"How could you be? And how could anyone take their own life?"

"Oh, I think I understand why, but I'm still angry at what he's done to my mother and me."

Lacey was at a loss as to what to say. "Were you and your father close?"

Preston sat still, as if in deep thought, before he answered. "I thought we were, but now I'm not too sure. We lived together, we worked in the same office, we golfed together, but now, I don't think we were close at all."

"Do you know why he killed himself?"

He nodded his head. "Yeah, because he was a coward and couldn't face the mess he got himself into by gambling away a fortune."

"Maybe he couldn't face letting you and your mother down," she suggested.

"Maybe, but trying to get the estate in order, and protecting my mother has certainly made me grow up in a hurry. I hope she'll never have to know what he did to our finances before he killed himself."

"She doesn't know?"

"No, and I hope she never will."

"Preston, you should tell her what's going on. People are going to talk. She'll find out one day, and it'd be better coming from you."

"No." He pressed his lips together.

"You'll be sorry," she predicted.

"Thank you for your sage advice, but I can handle my own life. I managed thirty-two years without your wisdom to guide me."

Lacey pressed her lips together and clasped her knees tightly to her chest.

"I don't want to hurt my mother. That house has been in her family for generations, and he actually took out a second mortgage on it to throw away gambling. I can't let her lose her home."

"Maybe it's more important to you than it is to her," Lacey murmured.

"I'll tell you another thing I've discovered," Preston continued, either ignoring her comment, or not hearing it. "I've found that our friends are fair-weather friends, almost all of them. Only Henry and his family have stood by me."

"Maybe your friends don't know what to say to you." Lacey took pity on him again. Preston had been through a lot. "When my father walked out, everyone avoided us—the neighbors, his parents, their friends. It wasn't until years later that some of them confessed they hadn't known what to say to us, they felt so badly."

"I think our so-called friends just don't want to associate with us anymore in case they are tainted in some way with the Rockwell scandal." He stood up and stretched. "If you want to go below and take a bath or something, I promise not to peek."

"I've had my last public showing, thank you, and last bath. I'm going to bed." She got up and went down into the cabin.

"You'll be pretty gamey in about three days," Preston warned.

"I know. By watching, not to mention smelling, you." And with that, she slammed the door. She crawled into her berth and lay there staring at the ceiling for a good two hours before finally falling into a fitful sleep.

Lacey's eyes flew open when she heard the splash. She could tell it was still dark, and her first thought was that Preston had fallen overboard. She hurried on deck, and saw his head bobbing in the moonlit water.

He was taking a swim. She could make out a small pile of something near the deck chair, and tiptoed over to find his shorts and underwear, and one of Henry's towels. She grinned to herself, gathered his clothes up and hid them on the cabin steps. Then she sat quietly in the deck chair with the towel, and waited.

After swimming several laps around the *Stud Muffin,* Preston pulled himself up over the side of the sailboat. He shook himself off and reached for the towel. Lacey wished she could better see his face as he frantically began searching for his clothes in the semi-darkness.

"Looking for this?" she finally asked.

Preston jumped as if he had backed into a hot poker and turned to face her. "I didn't see you there."

"I know." Lacey swallowed. In the low glow of the lights, with the sheen of water clinging to his skin, he looked like a Greek god. Perfectly proportioned in every way. Her eyes strayed irresistibly towards his genitals.

"Taking inventory?" Preston asked wryly.

"I wanted you to know how it felt to be stared at," she blurted.

"Ah, but I don't mind at all. Stare away." He flexed his muscles and Lacey giggled.

"Do you want the towel?" she asked, dangling the towel temptingly from her fingers.

"Maybe."

"Come and get it."

Preston stood still. "Lacey, give me the towel or you'll be sorry."

She had just decided he wasn't going to try and get the towel, when he closed the distance between them in two long strides, grabbed the towel from her and pulled her close.

"I told you to give me the towel," he whispered, and lowered his lips onto hers.

Lacey realized with striking clarity where what he was doing could lead. She wasn't ready for another physical relationship, but it was getting pretty obvious that Preston was. She could feel him harden against her.

She pushed against his shoulders with her fists, though not very hard, but he continued kissing her, and she slowly relaxed. They were deep, passionate kisses. He continued kissing her lips, then moved down to her neck and under her ear, leaving warm, moist spots on her skin with his lips and tongue. She felt goosebumps rise on her body and a quickening in her belly.

"Preston," she breathed.

He abruptly stopped and looked down at her. "What?" The poor lighting made both their expressions unreadable.

"We should stop. This isn't a good idea."

Preston's arms dropped from her and he carefully took the towel and draped it around his middle as Lacey turned and stumbled below.

Lacey could tell when she awoke the next morning, that the boat was moving. She didn't rush out on deck, because she really didn't want to face Preston yet. She went into the head and brushed her teeth and hair, and then started some water boiling for coffee and tea. She took her time, toasting several slices of bread and spreading them liberally with peanut butter. After delaying as much as possible, she took Preston's coffee and some peanut butter toast up to him.

He looked up, but didn't smile. "Thank you," he muttered.

Lacey went down to get her tea and toast, wondering if he was angry with her. They sat in silence eating the toast, sipping their drinks, and generally avoiding eye contact.

After they finished their breakfast, the silence became unbearable. Finally they both took deep breaths, and Preston asked her how she had slept just as Lacey commented on the fact the wind was blowing. They both grinned and the tension was broken.

"When did the wind pick up?" asked Lacey.

"Daybreak. It's not exactly the perfect direction like it has been, but we're still making good time. We already lost the *Filthy Rich* this morning."

"Great. Are we in the lead?"

"I'm not sure right now. I haven't been able to pick up anything on this radio since the night before last." He didn't want to get his hopes up, but he felt pretty confident they were ahead.

"How far are we from Bermuda?"

"Not very far. We should see it today, maybe even dock late tonight."

"What happens in Bermuda, anyway?"

"Each couple signs in at the Mangrove Bay Wharf and we stay on the island at the Cambridge Club. We leave for the return trip to Florida precisely forty-eight hours from the minute we land."

"Why do we have to stay forty-eight hours?"

"So the judges can assess the auxiliary engines and so we can rest up."

Lacey moaned. "I didn't bring any nice clothes for Bermuda. I didn't know we were staying. I thought we'd just sign in and leave."

"You'll notice that I didn't bring any clothes at all, but then I wasn't planning on dining, dancing, or sightseeing anyway."

"Where do we stay again?"

"At the Cambridge Club compound, in one of the cottages."

"Together?"

"It's common for the teams to stay together and I don't have enough cash to rent two separate cottages." Preston watched the play of emotions on her face. He was beginning to be able to read her moods and thoughts by her expressions. He wished the boat had been better lit last night so he could have seen the expression on her face as she looked his body over. "The cottage is bigger than this boat, Lacey, and I'll behave."

She gave him a quick smile. "I'm sorry. I guess I didn't expect this forty-eight hour layover. I hate not planing ahead."

"You could call your mother from there," he suggested, knowing the thought would make her happy.

"That's an idea. I know she's wondering what's going on."

"Why? Because the rigid Lacey did something spontaneous like go sailing on a whim?"

She looked sheepish "Well, something like that."

"I'll bet she's thrilled you're doing something fun."

"That's pretty observant of you. Am I really that rigid?"

"Well, I thought you were overly so at first. However, I can see that being in control, to a degree, is necessary to survival. I'm learning from you." He glanced down at his watch. "I'm going to get some sleep. Let me know when and if you spot land." He disappeared below.

Lacey went and sat in the deck chair. She gave the compass a quick check, picked up her sailing book and began reading. She didn't want to let Preston down.

Seven

"What are you doing?" Preston shouted.

Lacey's eyes flew open, and to her horror, it was dusk. She must have been asleep for hours. Preston's face was in hers and he was yelling at her like a drill sergeant.

"Do you notice anything, Lacey? Like maybe we're on the wrong side of the island? That's the St. David's Head light—on the eastern side of the island! I asked you to call me when you spotted land. I can't believe you fell asleep at the wheel!"

"Stop screaming at me. I'm sorry. I didn't fall asleep on purpose." Her voice quivered. She sat up straight and looked to her left. They were almost past the island, though it was still quite a distance away. "Just turn left and we'll go around, no problem."

"Starboard," he gritted. "And the sailing route has always been to go around the island on the western side first." He ran his fingers through his hair.

"Is there a rule against going around on the eastern side?" she asked hopefully.

He looked down at her and frowned. "The rules. I'll check the rules." He disappeared below.

Lacey was quaking in her chair. What if there was a rule against what they were positioned to do? It would take hours to backtrack and circle the island the other way. She crossed her fingers and waited.

He finally came back on deck. "There's no rule against what we're going to do. I want you to turn the wheel while I adjust the sails."

She stood, untied the rope anchoring the wheel, and waited for his orders, holding onto the wheel with a deathlike grip.

"Turn starboard until I tell you to stop." She did as he instructed as he began to turn the winch that controlled the boom. The huge mainsail ponderously turned almost an entire forty-five degrees before he quit. "Okay, stop turning, and hold it steady."

He went to the rear of the boat and put the smaller sail in the same position. They began to move more rapidly straight towards the right side of the island. He pulled out the charts, and glanced up. "You can get some rest now. You obviously need it."

She hurried downstairs and shut the cabin door. He was acting as if she had deliberately sabotaged the trip. She couldn't believe she had fallen asleep any more than he could. She sat on her bunk and looked around. On Preston's bunk was an array of papers.

Curiosity got the best of her, so after glancing at the door, she picked them all up and flipped rapidly through the stack. She found the transfer of ownership papers for the *Stud Muffin,* the copies of their entry forms, and a six-page document entitled "The Ridgeway Yacht Club Race Rules." This she took to her bunk, and after settling comfortably on her stomach, she began to read.

* * *

Thirty-five minutes later, she stomped back on deck, her face as red as her chopped-off hair. Preston was holding tightly to the wheel and looking intently ahead. Lacey waved the rule book in front of him.

"Guess what I just found out, Mr. Rockwell?"

"I'm busy right now," he said tersely.

"You lied to me. You told me the winner got five thousand dollars."

"The winner does get five thousand. Get out of my line of vision."

"Yes, the winner does get five thousand, plus another one hundred ninety-five thousand!" she shouted. "Preston, the prize is two hundred thousand dollars! You only offered me twenty-five hundred!"

"Which, in the course of twelve hours, you upped to five grand, if we win," he reminded her.

"But Preston, if we win I deserve more than only five. I should at least get half. I've been helping you a lot, you said so." Her hands were on her hips again.

"But Lacey," he mimicked, "I thought money wasn't everything to you. Isn't that what you said? And we have a signed contract. You agreed to come with me for twenty-five hundred, five grand if we win which we probably won't do now that you fell asleep, and that's exactly what you'll get. Leave me alone."

Lacey stared at him with narrowed eyes before returning below. She threw the papers on his bunk and flung herself on hers. He had shown no remorse whatsoever about lying to her.

Preston took a deep breath and clutched the wheel. He had explained to her that his father had mortgaged the family home, and he wasn't going to lose it for his mother's sake. And she had pretended money wasn't important. Maybe Lacey wasn't that different from everyone else, after all.

Lights were visible on the island as they rounded to the north side. They were to harbor at the Mangrove Bay Wharf which was on the western side of the island, and it would take several hours in the waning breeze to reach it. He was glad Lacey stayed below, even if it meant he had to do a lot of running back and forth to adjust the sails. It was also good they were going to stay in Bermuda at a time she was angry with him; it would eliminate any repetition of the night before, when he had momentarily lost his head and gone too far.

He signaled the Bermuda sea patrol station at Fort St. Catherine. He knew he'd need proof to the committee that he had indeed passed by this side of the island. He couldn't face disqualification. When the small patrol cutter pulled up nearby, he shouted out his dilemma, and they were more than happy to confirm his boat registration and to follow the *Stud Muffin* to the north side of the island. Lacey never even came out to see what the hullabaloo was about.

Three hours later, within sight of the wharf, Preston called for Lacey to come up and hold the wheel while he lowered the sails. She quietly complied, until he jerked the wheel from her and headed towards the lights visible in the small quiet bay. She took a deep breath, and inhaled the odor of honeysuckle and roses, and wondered what daylight would reveal. She dejectedly returned below and began packing her gear into her duffel bag. He yelled for her again, minutes later, to come out and grab one of the bollards. She guessed that he meant the poles holding up the docks. He ran forward and secured the bow line to one of several cleats available at the pier.

"You docked at 0110 hours, Preston. We were getting worried," said a deep, tired voice from the darkened dock. Preston recognized it at once. Mr. Reese, Henry's father, had waited up for them.

"We're okay. We just made a slight miscalculation." Preston secured all the lines and turned to see a pathetic Lacey standing with duffel bag in hand. "Come on, I'll help you up." He threw her duffel bag onto the dock and lifted her effortlessly up onto the dock.

"Thank you," Lacey mumbled.

"I'm sorry to say you're last, Preston. The other contestants arrived between 1900 and 2400 hours."

"We came around the eastern side of the island, Mr. Reese," explained Preston. Lacey waited for him to blame her.

The man slapped Preston on the back. "No rule against that. Could even mean you're first. Does anyone know you came that way?" the man frowned.

"I thought of that. I signaled at the Bermuda sea patrol station at Fort St. Catherine. They sent a small cutter out to check my flags and all, but when they realized I was a contestant, they didn't stop me, or board."

Lacey looked at him in amazement. She hadn't been aware of another boat, or of any of these events. She hoped he wasn't lying.

Mr. Reese laughed. "I always knew you were clever, boy. I'll have to tell the racing committee what you did so they don't question you setting out in the opposite direction of everyone else, and I'm sure they'll check on your story." He squinted his eyes down the pier. The lights were spaced so that large pockets of darkness existed. "That's peculiar. Henry has been hanging around the pier all day waiting for you. I guess he got discouraged and left." He clapped Preston on the shoulder again, and Lacey was thankful for Preston's sake that his sunburn had healed. "I'll buzz into the clubhouse and ask one of the houseboys to take you to your cottage."

He disappeared into the tiny building built on the end of the dock, returning a few minutes later. "I had Henry paged at the bar, too. He has some things for you."

A young man in uniform ran down the pier and quickly took Lacey's duffel bag from her and led them rapidly onto the lush grounds of the compound. Lacey couldn't wait until daylight to see if everything looked as good as it smelled. She tripped several times on the gravel path, but she attributed it to fatigue and sea legs, more than clumsiness. Preston never once tried to catch her, or help her keep her balance.

Finally they arrived at a small cottage, and the houseboy opened the door with a flourish and flipped on the lights. The brightness momentarily blinded them both, but Lacey could make out a small comfortable living room, decorated in shades of peach, white, and yellow. It was instantly comforting to her.

After waiting a disappointing few minutes for a tip that wasn't forthcoming, the boy walked off and left them alone. Lacey put down her bag and walked through the cottage, opening doors leading to a small kitchenette, two bedrooms, and a bathroom. When she walked into the bathroom, she let loose a shriek.

Preston, who had been opening the cabinets and refrigerator, hoping for some food, raced into the bathroom to find Lacey staring at the mirror, a look of horror on her face.

"What's wrong?"

She turned to him. "Why didn't you tell me I looked like this?"

"Like what?"

"My hair! It looks awful" She stared back into the mirror and he was shocked to see tears forming in her eyes.

"It just needs to be trimmed a little."

Lacey didn't move and it was Preston's turn to take pity on her. He put his hands on her shoulders and pushed her into the living room. "Get your duffel bag, take a nice hot shower, and crawl into bed. Things will look different to you after you've had some rest."

She slowly took her bag and walked into the bathroom and shut the door with a click. There was a knock at the front door, and Preston hurried to answer it.

"Pres, Dad told me you may be in first place." Henry pushed into the cottage carrying an obviously heavy box. "I brought everything you need. Sorry I couldn't get to you before you left Palm Beach." He put down the box, and stood up, taking a breath. "Wow, Preston, you look like hell."

Preston grinned. "Thanks, Henry, old pal." He peered into the box. "Please tell me you brought me some clothes."

Henry smiled and nodded. "When I went to your apartment, I noticed your suitcase sitting by the door, so I knew you'd forgotten it. I brought everything I could think of, or remember you said. Food, clothes, sheets, paper towels, toilet paper, paper plates, trash bags, flashlights, matches, dish detergent, disposable razors, your tux . . ."

Preston interrupted. "You can take the tux back with you."

"What about the party tomorrow night?"

"I'm not going, Henry. All I want is a change of clothes and clean underwear." He pulled at his filthy jeans shorts. "And I'm throwing these away tomorrow."

Henry looked around. "Where's your partner? What's her name—Lori?"

"Lacey," Preston corrected. "She's taking a shower."

"Did you guys, you know, do anything?"

"Henry, how can anyone race and make love at the same time? We sailed in shifts and barely saw each other."

"Oh." Henry sounded disappointed. "By the way, Rodney Fleming thinks he's winning. He's been bragging at the clubhouse bar all evening."

Preston laughed. "Won't he be surprised? I may have come into Mangrove Bay last, but I'll beat him back out to sea by about four hours."

"Cynthia isn't staying with him, if you're curious," Henry offered.

"I'm not." Preston set his lips together tightly.

"She rented a separate cottage when they got to shore." Henry waited, but Preston didn't speak.

The bathroom door cracked open, and Lacey peeked out. "Oh," she said when she saw Henry.

"Don't mind me. I'm leaving. You two need your rest." Henry headed for the cottage door and winked at Preston. "It's not too late, you know."

Preston pushed him out and shut the door in time to see one of the bedroom doors close. He decided to shower, shave, and order room service. He wanted meat, potatoes, vegetables and a huge dessert, and maybe a glass or two of wine.

Lacey listened as the water began to run for Preston's shower. She towel-dried her hair, and decided she couldn't bear to climb into any of her damp clothes again. Her hair curled around her face as she brushed it dry, and she crawled under the clean fresh sheets with delight and fell promptly asleep.

Sunshine sneaking into the room through the cracks in the closed shutters woke her up. She pushed aside the sheets and stretched, deciding to put on her bathing suit while she figured out some way to get her clothes cleaned. The other bedroom door was closed, so she assumed Preston was still asleep. To her gratification, she found a small washer and dryer tucked in a closet off the kitchenette. She immediately started a load of laundry with the small complimentary bottle of detergent and fabric softener, and wrapped one of the large bathroom towels around her waist before she left the cottage.

She stepped outside, in awe of the lush, sculptured surroundings. Every shrub was shaped to perfection, and flowers bloomed from every corner and along the sidewalks. As her nose had assured her last night, honeysuckle abounded, twisting itself in every possible nook and cranny. Every tree held several hanging baskets of ferns, and she wished she had brought her camera.

Each of the cottages was painted a pastel shade of pink with light blue shutters, and further up the path she spotted a larger, stucco building painted a deep rose with turquoise shutters. The clubhouse, she decided. She managed to find her way up the path to the entrance of the marina. She hurried down the pier and found the *Stud Muffin* at the end of a long line of sailboats.

She carefully jumped on board and looked into the water to see tiny colorful fish darting between the pilings. Reluctantly she went into the cabin. Here she stripped both bunks of all linens, gathered all of Henry's grubby towels, and pulled the whole mess out on deck. She had just managed to bundle it all into one of the blankets, when someone called to her.

"Lacey!"

She looked up to see Rodney weaving his way down the pier. "When did you two get in last night?"

"About one in the morning." She struggled to drag her bundle over to the edge of the boat.

"You know you aren't going to win, don't you?"

"Rodney, you and I have nothing to say to one another. Besides, you're drunk."

He stood up straight. "I'm not drunk," he said, promptly collapsing against one of the tarred poles holding up the pier.

"Look. Help me onto the pier with this stuff." Lacey was losing patience with him.

He reached for the bundle and almost dropped it

into the water. She scrambled onto the pier and quickly removed the bundle from his grasp. "Go to your cottage, Rodney, and sleep it off."

"You're nice, Lacey. Do you want your job back? I'll talk to my dad," he slurred.

Lacey promptly shook her head. "No, Rodney. But thanks. You better get off the dock before you fall off."

"I am feeling a little dizzy, Lacey. Could you help me back to my cottage?"

She narrowed her eyes at him, wondering if he really felt bad. "Put your hand on my arm and steady yourself. I've got to carry this stuff." She shifted her load to her other hip. "Come on!"

Rodney grabbed her arm with his left hand and slung his right arm around her shoulders. "I've been a jerk, haven't I? Cynthia says I'm a spoiled brat. You like me though, don't you?"

Lacey didn't answer. She just wished he would go away.

"Lacey," he said, plaintively.

She turned her face to his, trying not to gag at his liquor-laden breath. "What?" Before she knew what he was doing, he had clamped his mouth securely over hers. She dropped her bundle and pushed him away with all her strength. He went backward and balanced for a harrowing moment on the edge of the pier before falling into the bay with a splash. She peered over the edge and saw him sitting and sputtering in less than a foot of water. She picked up her bundle, only to have it swept immediately from her arms by Preston.

She blushed and wondered how much he had witnessed. He looked at her and grinned. "That just about makes up for falling asleep yesterday, Ms. Campbell. Gosh, I wish I had a video camera. The expression on Rodney's face when he balanced on the pier edge was priceless." She heard a low rumble from his throat and soon he emitted a deep, masculine laugh. "You have spunk, Lacey, I'll give you that."

Lacey smiled at his laughter. He had a beautiful laugh, and it was a shame he didn't use it more. "I just did what I had to do, Mr. Rockwell. You'd do well to remember that." She took the bundle from him and disappeared into their cottage.

Was that a warning not to kiss her anymore? He followed her inside to find her transferring the wet clothes to the dryer and loading the sheets into the washer. "Have you had breakfast?" he asked.

"No. I don't have anything clean to wear yet."

"After your clothes dry, let's go on up to the clubhouse and get our share of the complimentary breakfast."

She put her hands to her hair and frowned.

"Henry brought us a pair of scissors. Do you want to even up your hair?"

Lacey looked gratefully at him. "Could you even up the back for me?"

Preston looked momentarily disconcerted, but agreed at her look of obvious dejection. They went out on the patio and he pulled a lawn chair up while Lacey wrapped one of the cottage bath towels around her neck after wetting her hair.

Preston carefully measured her hair from her head with his fingers and cut the ragged edges evenly. He pushed her head down and cut around the top of her slender neck. When he squatted beside her to cut the ends near her face, he noticed, feeling somewhat foolish, that she had the prettiest ears, with tiny freckles inside the pink shell-like interior. He felt beads of sweat form on his upper lip as he concentrated on cutting her hair and tried to forget how attractive she was. Finally he stepped away, and said, "Finished."

Her eyes flew open and she hurried into the bathroom to wash her hair. Preston heard the clothes dryer stop and went to retrieve the clothing before they wrinkled. He pulled out several colorful tops and shorts which he recalled seeing Lacey wear during the trip, and folded them carefully. He then pulled a bra out and quickly looked at the tag to see what size she wore. 34C. A good size, he thought. Next came the silk bikinis in all colors. Funny, she had looked like a cotton panty girl to him.

"What are you doing?" Lacey asked from the bathroom door.

Preston willed himself not to look guilty and answered nonchalantly, "Folding laundry."

Lacey shrugged before sitting back on the patio to dry her hair in the sun. Preston took out the sheets and put them in the dryer, and started a load of Henry's beach towels, then he joined Lacey on the patio.

"Who taught you to do laundry?" she asked without opening her eyes.

"I do have my own apartment, you know." He didn't bother to mention that until he had been forced to let the staff go, he had always taken his laundry home and had his mother's housekeeper, Florence, do it.

"I'm hungry." She lifted her head from the back

of her chair. "Let me dress, and I'll be ready to go."
She streaked into the kitchen and slammed into the
bedroom with her arms full of clothes. He had
dressed for breakfast earlier in jeans, deck shoes, and
a light pink golf shirt.

Lacey entered the room in less than ten minutes.
She had fluffed her hair, and put on a touch of brown
eye shadow to bring out her eyes. She had on a bright
yellow tank top, with green, red, blue, white, and yellow Hawaiian print shorts, and white canvas slip-ons.
"You did a great job on my hair." She ran her fingers
up through the natural curls.

"Thanks. Come on, I'm starving." He grabbed her
hand and practically dragged her out of the cottage
and down the white gravel path.

When they were almost to the clubhouse, Henry
emerged from one of the cottages and joined them.

"I was wondering, Pres, if you and Lacey would
like to go sightseeing later this morning. They have
mopeds here for the guests."

Preston saw Lacey's eyes light up. They paused outside the clubhouse while Henry waited patiently for
Preston to answer.

"I have to check all the riggings and load the supplies. I don't have time for playing around this year,"
he finally muttered.

Lacey looked down and Preston could sense her
disappointment; only a moron wouldn't have.

Henry turned to Lacey. "Would you like to come
with me? We could run over to Hamilton and eat
lunch in one of the pubs."

Preston looked sharply at Lacey. She was smiling
one of her rare dimpled smiles at Henry. He felt a
pang of some emotion he was unfamiliar with, know-

ing only that it made him want to strangle Henry, and have Lacey smile that way at him.

Before he knew what he was saying, he blurted, "Oh, we'll go with you. We can get things settled when we get back."

Lacey and Henry looked at him in surprise.

As they entered the dining room, everyone turned and stared, just as Lacey had feared. After a moment of silence, they resumed their meals, but continued to slant looks at the crew of the *Stud Muffin* and Henry.

"We're the topic of every conversation, I bet," Preston whispered in her ear. He pulled her towards a table on the terrace overlooking the ocean. "Order anything you want. It's on the yacht club tab."

Lacey picked up the menu and gasped at the prices. She lowered it and whispered, "Are you sure?"

Henry looked at them in speculation over the top of his menu.

"Yes. I promise. Won't cost us a penny," Preston assured her.

She looked at him and he wondered if she was thinking his promises weren't worth very much. He wished now he hadn't lied to her about the prize money. She would probably never trust him again.

They both returned silently to their menus with Henry closing his and watching them both closely. When the waiter came, they ordered gargantuan breakfasts including everything they couldn't eat on the boat: waffles, eggs benedict, sausage and bacon.

They ate with relish, listening to Henry talk of the other racers and latest gossip.

As soon as they finished, Henry led them to the mopeds.

"Don't forget they drive on the left here, like in England."

"I won't remember that. Can I ride on the back of one of your mopeds?" Lacey asked worriedly.

"You can ride with me," offered Preston before Henry could answer.

They chose two yellow mopeds, and the attendant fitted them with safety helmets. Henry roared off first with a wave of his hand, and Lacey awkwardly settled behind Preston, putting her arms loosely around his waist.

"Better hold on tighter than that or you'll fall off."

Lacey tightened her hold and felt his warmth through the front of her shirt. Preston gunned the motor and roared out of the parking lot, trying to catch Henry. After she caught her breath, she began to drink in the scenery.

Bermuda was enchanting. The homes on the island had a picture postcard look with blinding white terraced roofs and pastel exteriors. They were all painted pink, pale green, powder blue, or peach, and surrounded by lush flowering vegetation: oleander, wisteria, gardenias and hibiscus.

The two mopeds raced along Middle Road down the center of the island. Preston delighted in hearing Lacey gasp in breathless wonder at the magnificent coastline views. Henry stopped at every roadside stand and shop, and Preston and Henry watched her look longingly at the colorful pottery, cedar clocks, dolls, and miniature cottages, and sample the various perfumes. Henry tried to buy her everything he thought she liked, but she refused to let him spend a penny. Preston found himself admiring her for that.

When they reached the outskirts of Hamilton, Henry skidded to a stop in front of a small building called "Reggie's Pub." Since they were still full from breakfast, they just ordered fruit drinks.

"Why are the roofs all white?" asked Lacey.

"That's how the islanders get their drinking water, through catching the water from their roofs after a rain," answered Henry.

"I haven't seen anyone in bathing suits, either. In Palm Beach, all the tourists stay in their suits."

"Bermuda is much more conservative than the U.S.," continued Henry, obviously enjoying her attention. "Bathing suits are for swimming only, and you won't see any short shorts, either. Bermudian's really are a little prudish."

Preston was tired of being ignored, so he glanced pointedly at his watch. "We better he heading back," he suggested.

"We've only been gone less than two hours!" protested Lacey and Henry in unison.

"I have work to do on the *Stud Muffin,* remember?"

"All work and no play makes Preston a dull boy," murmured Henry.

Preston stood up. "Lacey?"

"I can take her back," offered Henry.

Preston frowned at Lacey. "Are you coming?"

She glanced at Henry and then back to Preston. "I'll go back with Henry," she said timidly.

"Fine." Preston stalked out of the pub and they listened as the moped roared off.

"Uh-oh," said Henry.

"I know. He can be so sweet, and then turn into a bear, but I want to enjoy Bermuda. Who knows when I'll get back here?"

Henry patted her shoulder. "Don't worry about it."

They left the pub and Lacey settled behind Henry. Luckily Preston had left her the helmet. But all too soon, she felt obligated to suggest that Henry take her back to the cottage compound.

"There's a saltwater pool on the other side of the compound. It's Olympic-size," Henry told her as she climbed off the moped.

Lacey's eyes brightened. She had only been swimming once so far, and having been perpetually surrounded by water for the last few days, that didn't seem very fair. "Thanks. I love to swim."

She waved good-bye to Henry and entered her cottage. She went immediately over to fold sheets and transfer the laundry in the machines. She put on her bathing suit and took one of the cottage towels with her, plus the sunblock lotion and a pair of sunglasses.

Touring the island had been fun, but somehow, Preston's face had been in the back of her mind all morning. She had found herself wishing it had been his back she had clung to rather than Henry's throughout the rest of the morning and afternoon, though Henry was very sweet and nice. And that was puzzling. Why would she rather cling to a grumpy Preston than a kind Henry? She sighed and went outside.

In no time, she found the pool and picked a lounge chair off to the side to deposit her stuff on before walking over, diving into the water, and doing soothing laps around the huge pool. She swam until she almost went numb, and climbed out of the pool, shaking her arms and hair free of water. She smoothed on the lotion, positioned her sunglasses, and began to doze off.

The sound of a chair scraping on cement awoke her. Someone was moving next to her, and she prayed it wasn't Rodney. She barely opened her eyes to see a woman puttering around the chair before she finally lay down and turned to Lacey with a smile and extended hand.

"Hello. I'm Cynthia Starling," the woman said.

Eight

Lacey timidly extended her hand and shook the other woman's. Cynthia put on her sunglasses, removed her wrap to reveal a scrap of fluorescent pink bikini, and languidly stretched her impossibly long legs out on the lounge chair. Lacey could see why Preston had been attracted to this woman. She had looks, style, and a natural grace. Lacey decided she hated her.

"You looked lonely, so I thought I'd join you." She turned to face Lacey. "I hope you don't mind." It was a statement more than a question. Lacey shook her head, at a total loss for words. "Also, I think Rodney will stay as far away from you as possible, and I hope sitting next to you will keep him away from me, too." She gave a deep, throaty laugh. "God, I'd love to have seen his face when you pushed him off the pier."

Lacey was astounded that Cynthia knew what she had done to Rodney. Had Preston met her and told her? The idea of Cynthia and Preston meeting and talking, or doing anything else together, caused her stomach to churn.

"I thought you liked Rodney," Lacey ventured.

"Until this trip I did. He's been obnoxious. I wish now I had sailed with Pres."

Lacey cringed at her use of the nickname. "Why didn't you?" She knew it was none of her business, but she had a damnably curious nature at times.

"He began acting so distant and tense, not like the Pres I've always known, and Rodney was so attentive and charming . . . well, you know how it is sometimes." She gestured into the air. "I think I thought Pres would beg me to come back or something, but then I heard from Rodney he had found you for a partner." Lacey listened for a sneer in Cynthia's voice, but heard none.

"How are you and Pres doing?"

Lacey was glad she was wearing sunglasses, to hide the suspicion she felt from all of Cynthia's chatter. "We're doing fine."

"Rodney says you worked for him at one time," Cynthia stated.

Lacey felt her defenses go up. "I worked for Fleming Inns, actually, in Seattle."

"Seattle? How on earth did you end up in Florida, sailing in a race?"

"I took a job transfer as kitchen manager at the Palm Beach Fleming Inn, but Rodney doesn't treat his employees fairly or very well, so I quit," answered Lacey.

Cynthia let go another low, throaty laugh. "He's such a jerk. I hope you quit with a flourish."

"I turned him in to the Palm Beach Health Department." Lacey grinned, despite herself.

"How long had you worked for Fleming Inns?" asked Cynthia.

"Eight years."

"What will you do when you get back to Palm Beach?"

"I guess it depends on this race, but win or lose, I'd like to get a job and stay in Florida."

They lay in companionable silence. Lacey thought Cynthia had fallen asleep until she surprised her by speaking.

"Are you coming to the party tonight?"

"What party?"

Cynthia lifted her head and faced her. "The party for all the contestants?"

Lacey felt her face heat up. "I didn't know about any party, and besides, I . . . I didn't bring any nice clothes," she stammered.

Cynthia shot out of her chair and grabbed her things. "For heaven's sake, you should have told me sooner. Come on."

Startled, Lacey stood and gathered her towel and lotion. "Where are we going?"

"To my cottage. I might have a dress or two that would fit you."

Lacey hesitated. "What about Rodney? I don't think he'd want me in your cottage."

Cynthia laughed. "After five days trapped on a boat with him, do you honestly think I'd want him in my cottage? Come on."

Lacey reluctantly followed, still uncertain as to Cynthia's motives. When they arrived at the cottage, Cynthia rushed into the bedroom and came back with her arms full of evening dresses.

"You brought all these with you on the boat?" Lacey asked in wonder.

Cynthia looked at her in amazement. "Of course not. Mummy and Daddy brought them to me this morning."

"Maybe this isn't a good idea, Cynthia. You're

much taller than I am and I wouldn't have time to hem anything. Also, I don't have evening shoes."

Cynthia ignored her as she draped the dresses over the sofa and stood back with the long red fingernail of her index finger tapping her teeth.

"Preston doesn't have anything to wear," Lacey added for good measure.

Cynthia didn't even look over. "Nonsense. He's usually the life of the party at these events. I assure you he has a tux somewhere."

Lacey chewed her bottom lip in vexation. She hadn't seen anything but those filthy jeans on Preston until today. Maybe Henry had brought him formal wear, and he was just being nice about not telling her because he knew she had nothing to wear. Or was he planning to attend the party without her? She felt a rush of grim determination. No way was he going without her.

"Look. I wear this as a cocktail dress, but on you it would almost be full length." Cynthia was holding up a beaded gown in graduated shades of green with a slit up the side.

"Um." It looked mighty risqué to her.

"Try it on," Cynthia insisted. "Over your suit. It's dry, isn't it?"

"Yes, but—"

"No buts." Cynthia shoved her towards the bedroom. "Now go."

Lacey still hesitated. Cynthia put her hands on her hips. "It's three o'clock, Lacey."

Lacey turned and hurried into the bedroom, clutching the dress. It dawned on her that she hadn't worn a watch in days, and hadn't cared about the time since she left shore in Palm Beach, until this very minute. She had lived by the clock for so long, it gave her a ridiculous sense of freedom not to wear one, but right now, time was of the essence.

She pulled on the gown and struggled to zip it up, when Cynthia burst into the room, and completed the task for her. She stood back and looked critically at Lacey. "I think it will do. It's about an inch from the floor in back, and the slit only goes above your knee. It goes so high on me, I have to wear a G-sting. Now shoes. You wear a size 6, am I right?"

Lacey nodded her head. Cynthia tapped her foot impatiently on the carpet. "I know! Mummy! She's a size six, and I'm sure she brought every shoe she owns. She always does!" She rushed over and hurried Lacey out of the dress.

"You go to your place and get cleaned up. I'll be right over with some shoes."

"But—"

"Hurry! It takes me hours to get ready, and the party is at eight." She pushed Lacey unceremoniously out the door. Lacey walked slowly back to the cottage. Lacey felt naive and gauche in the other woman's presence, yet Cynthia had done nothing to make her feel that way.

She entered the cottage, folded the laundry, and started the last load in the dryer. She was headed for the shower, when there was a sharp knock at the door. She opened it to find Cynthia, who thrust two bags at her and winked. "I threw in some stockings. See you tonight at the clubhouse."

Lacey stood holding the bags, staring blankly at the empty doorway, before she remembered that Preston could return at any minute. She hurried into her bedroom and closed the door. Slowly she opened the bags and removed each item. The shoes were gold, matching the gold beads sewn randomly into the dress, which glittered glamorously and invitingly through the clear plastic bag. She put everything in the closet, and went in to take a long, hot shower.

Preston entered the cottage, sweaty and hot, wanting nothing more than a shower himself. He was determined to get dinner over with early before the yacht club crowd started to gather in their party finery. He didn't intend to give them a chance to snub him because of his financial troubles. He stopped short at the bathroom door. Damn, she had beat him to it. The dryer buzzed and he went over and began folding the sheets, thinking the trip back to Palm Beach would be infinitely more pleasant with the clean bedding and the other supplies Henry had brought.

The water stopped running and Lacey soon popped out of the bathroom, wrapped in a towel. "Hi." She hesitated, and then decided to give him a opening to tell her about the party. "What should I wear to dinner?"

"Just shorts. We'll probably be the first ones there, and the first ones out, anyway."

"Why?"

"Why what?"

"Why won't anyone else be there?"

He didn't know what to say. Not only did he want to avoid the party, he didn't want her to feel badly that she had nothing to wear. "Because this crowd eats late," he said lamely.

"Oh." She turned and disappeared into her room. He took his shower and slipped on a pair of shorts and went out to sit on the patio to let his hair dry in the afternoon sun. He closed his eyes and was dozing soundly within minutes.

Locked in her room, Lacey carefully applied the eye shadow and mascara she had brought with her in her cosmetic bag. Why she had thought to bring make-up, and not pajamas or a nightgown, she didn't know. Her hair dried in natural swirls around her face and she applied just the tiniest amount of blush over each checkbone. She slid on the stockings and lifted the dress over her head. The fabric was heavy with beads, but she was willing to bear the weight in exchange for the beauty of the garment. She shimmied into the sheath and reached back to zip it. It took several minutes of cursing and struggling before she got the zipper up completely. After slipping on the shoes, she stood in front of the wooden full-length mirror.

She gasped when she saw her reflection. She felt like Cinderella. The shades of graduated green on her dress made her green eyes large and luminous. The slit revealed an intriguing amount of leg, and the strapless top revealed alarming portions of her rounded breasts. She walked carefully to the door, not accustomed to such high heels, and swallowed in sudden panic when her hand touched the knob. What if Cynthia had worn this dress before on a date with Preston?

Her clammy hand slipped off the knob as she tried to turn it, but on her second attempt, it opened. She peered down the hall and into the living room, but Preston was nowhere to be found. She cautiously opened his bedroom door, but both his bed and room were empty. Trying not to panic, she went over to the patio door and looked out, to find him asleep with his mouth open, in one of the two chairs. She walked out and shook him gently.

"Preston?"

Preston's eyes fluttered open and he looked up at her. He sat up with a jerk, and gazed at her from head to toe as she stepped instinctively away.

She swallowed nervously, unable to tell what he was thinking. "Well?" she finally asked.

"Well, wow! Where did you get that dress?"

"Cynthia lent it to me." She searched his face for a reaction, but only saw the puzzlement she, too, felt at Cynthia's generosity.

"Lacey, you look beautiful. Gorgeous. Delectable. All this for dinner?"

"No, for the party after."

Preston closed his eyes. "I wasn't planning to attend the party."

"Preston, please let's go. It will probably be my only chance ever to wear a beaded gown and mingle with money."

"Let me call Henry and tell him to bring over my tux," he said none too happily.

"Cynthia said you'd have a tux here on the island." Cynthia obviously knew Preston far better than she did. "She also said you were usually the life of the party."

"Lacey, when I was here before, I had no problems, no responsibilities. This year is different." He stood up and headed inside for the phone, leaving a perplexed Lacey on the patio. Had she forced him into something that would make him feel uncomfortable? Was this what Cynthia had wanted? She sat gingerly down in the chair and rested her chin on her hand.

Why couldn't they have just kept sailing and skipped this whole Bermuda stop?

Preston took one more look at himself in the mirror. It seemed like years since he had worn this tux, but he guessed it was only seven or so months ago. He patted his hair into place, and went into the living room.

Lacey was bedazzled when she saw him. He was devastatingly, drop-dead handsome in the stark black and white of the formal wear. Her heart plummeted. No man this good-looking was going to ever want someone as ordinary as herself.

Preston immediately noticed how crestfallen she seemed moments after he had entered the room, and he searched his memory for anything he might have said to give her that lost look.

"You miss your family, don't you?" he ventured.

"Yes," she lied.

"Well, let's go on and eat dinner now, and we'll stay for the party. I'm famished."

Lacey put her hand in the crook of his proffered arm and berated herself for having romantic daydreams. A few moonlit kisses didn't mean anything in today's world, and she was probably overreacting to think they were important. Preston would probably have acted the same towards any female partner he was confined with on a boat for days on end. She tried to maintain her balance on the graveled path to the clubhouse, but Preston had to reach over and save her twice from failing. His arms felt so warm and safe in the cool evening breeze.

There were few diners in the clubhouse. "We'll eat

low," Preston assured her, when she frowned at all he empty tables.

He ordered them both a Dark and Stormy and two hrimp cocktails.

"What on earth is a Dark and Stormy?" asked Lacey.

"It's a local drink made with black rum and ginger beer." When the waiter brought them their drinks, she watched fascinated as Preston picked his drink up and quaffed it in a few swallows. "Excellent!" he pronounced, before ordering another. When the waiter returned with another drink, Preston raised his glass in a toast. "To this year's winners of the Ridgeway Yacht Club race."

Lacey clinked her glass to his and hoped he was right and that they would win.

"Now tell me about you and Cynthia." His eyes drifted towards the gleaming dress or to her breasts, she wasn't sure which.

Lacey shrugged. "She came up to me at the pool and began talking, and when she heard we weren't attending the party, she offered me one of her dresses."

"It seems to me I remember that dress from somewhere, but she certainly didn't fill it out as well as you do."

Lacey flushed with pleasure. He quickly finished off his drink and waved to the waiter for another. She hoped his unexpected compliment hadn't just been the drinks talking.

"What else did Cynthia have to say?" he asked. Lacey shifted in her seat, uncomfortable with his profound interest in Cynthia.

"That Rodney was obnoxious and she wished she had sailed with you."

"I wished she had, too, dammit. Then I know I'd win. Did you know she was on the America's Cup team for the United States two years ago?"

The blood had drained from Lacey's face, but Preston hadn't noticed. He signaled the waiter and rattled off both orders to the waiter without asking her what she wanted.

"You aren't drinking your drink. Don't you care for it?" He was stabbing the tiny boiled shrimp in the cocktail sauce and eating them avidly.

She sat tight-lipped, in silence, staring sullenly at her silverware, and wanting beyond everything else, to pour her drink on Preston's head. Every time she felt herself begin to like the idiot, he did something to make her feel like dirt.

He drained his drink and began looking curiously around the room, his eyes darting from table to table, and then to the door. She wondered if he was waiting for Cynthia to enter the room. Lacey was contemplating calling her mother to send her airfare home from Bermuda, but her pride quelled any further thoughts in that direction.

Preston ordered himself another Dark and Stormy when the waiter served their Caesar salads. He began sloppily shoving the crisp leaves of dripping romaine lettuce into his mouth while Lacey pushed hers aimlessly around her salad plate.

Soon he was totally oblivious to everything but the entrance to the dining room. His eyes constantly wandered there, and she now felt sure he was waiting for Cynthia. She wished she'd never mentioned anything about what Cynthia had said.

Preston ate with abandon. He was hungry, having skipped lunch after their huge breakfast that morn-

ing. He was also anxious. What if no one spoke to
him? What if they all whispered behind his back? He
set down his fork on his now empty plate, and nervously fiddled with his bow tie, totally ignoring Lacey's presence.

The waiter swept away their dishes and served
them two bowls of Bermuda fish chowder. Preston
didn't hesitate to dig in. He was hallway through before he remembered to even put his napkin in his
lap. Soon the waiter had returned with two plates
bristling with spiny lobster. Lacey swallowed. To her
they had all the appeal of giant dead bugs, and her
appetite completely disappeared. The next time Preston managed to speak to her, it was to ask if she was
going to eat her lobster, and when she shook her
head, he lifted it onto his plate, and ate it, too.

By the time the waiter came to clear away dishes,
Preston had finished off both meals, and Lacey had
only eaten the soft center out of a roll. She hoped
he threw up all night from all the rich food and alcohol he had consumed. Couples had come in during their meal, pointedly ignoring Preston, and, after
eating, had drifted into the next room.

Lacey finally excused herself and went into the ladies' room to sit in one of the overstuffed chairs just
inside the door. If Cynthia thought Rodney was obnoxious, she should have watched Preston eat tonight.

When she finally returned to the table, Preston was
gone. Rather than embarrass herself by searching the
room for him, she went into the room where everyone else had gone earlier. It was a grand ballroom,
lit with two large chandeliers. A full orchestra sat at
the opposite end of the room.

"Lacey!" Henry appeared at her side. "Where's Pres?" he asked, looking over her head and then back down at her. "You look gorgeous." She knew by the admiring tone in his voice that he wasn't just being polite.

"Thanks. Preston is in his own world tonight. I'm not sure where he is."

"Poor old Pres. He's been through a lot, you know. I think he'll be okay, though." It sounded so similar to what everyone had said about her when her former fiancé had eloped with her stepsister that she felt a sudden empathy for Preston. But it had hurt when Preston said he wished Cynthia had sailed with him instead of her. Hard times didn't automatically allow bad manners.

The orchestra struck up a tune, and Henry bowed. "May I have this dance?"

Lacey smiled. "You may."

They slow danced around the floor with Henry making polite chatter throughout the whole dance. Lacey tried not to look around for Preston, but she did anyway. However Preston had apparently disappeared. When the orchestra switched to another song, she was asked to dance by another young man, who whisked her away before she could even answer. After each dance, she was surrounded by attractive men requesting the pleasure of dancing with her. She was overwhelmed, elated, and at the same time, bereft at Preston's abandonment. Cynthia spoke to her twice, but she, too, was whisked onto the dance floor as often as Lacey. At least she had the satisfaction of knowing Cynthia and Preston weren't together.

At eleven, she slipped out the door and found her way back to the cottage. She was exhausted, exhilarated, and furious at Preston for leaving her. She wished he could have seen all the men who had asked her to dance. She opened the door, and heard Preston growl from the dark interior.

"Where in the hell have you been?"

Nine

Lacey flipped on the light switch and was pleased to note Preston flinched and covered his eyes. He was sprawled on the tiny sofa, his jacket and tie laying on the floor, his shoes missing, and best of all, his face looked a sickly shade of green.

"I'd rather know where you've been, Mr. Rockwell."

"I was sitting at our table and you disappeared, so I came looking for you."

"You'll have to do better than that. I told you I had to go to the ladies' room, but I suppose you can't remember very much with everything you drank."

Preston pulled his arm up over the back of the sofa where it had been dangling, and Lacey saw his hand held a washcloth, which he promptly put over his eyes.

"I was worried about you," he said.

"That's a laugh. I'm willing to bet the measly twenty-five hundred I'm getting at the end of this race that you started feeling sick and went out into the bushes to throw up. Meanwhile, I spent all evening in the company of complete strangers, except for Henry, explaining to people that you had been sick on the trip, and were still feeling slightly ill."

"How many people really asked about me, Lacey?"

"Three. Cynthia, Henry, and Henry's dad," she said, suddenly feeling contrite and wishing there had been more.

"Three whole people."

Lacey took off her shoes and stood looking at the pathetic Preston.

Preston lifted the edge of the washcloth and peered at her. "What?" he asked.

"Nothing. Everything. You have got to be the most frustrating man I've ever met," she said as she swept past the sofa and disappeared into the bedroom with a loud slam of her door.

Preston winced at the noise and groaned. She certainly knew how to slam a door effectively. He had been violently sick for the last three hours. He pledged never to eat again. For someone who ceased partying and drinking six months ago, drinking Dark and Stormies had been an incredibly stupid move on his part. His stomach began roiling again, and he stumbled to the bathroom, his hand clamped tightly over his mouth.

In her room, Lacey wrapped the borrowed shoes in tissue paper and placed them in one of the bags. She threw down the stockings to wash out in the bathroom sink later and return to Cynthia. She reached up to unzip the dress, and was relieved when the zipper came down more easily than it went up, until it caught tightly in the material right between her shoulder blades. She stood before the mirror and twisted to get a better look, but the material of the dress was firmly caught. After ten minutes of struggling and cursing, she had no choice but to ask Preston to help, or sleep in the dress.

She opened her door to find the cottage in darkness and the living room empty. His bedroom door was shut. She went up to it and knocked softly. "Preston?" He didn't answer, so she knocked harder, anxious to get out of the dress. "Preston, I need your help."

"Go away," came the muffled answer.

"Preston, please do me this one favor, and I'll leave you alone." He didn't answer.

"You're being childish. I'm coming in." She pushed open the door and caught her foot in something laying on the floor. To Preston's chagrin, she turned on the bright ceiling light and saw his evening clothes scattered everywhere about the room. He hunkered further under the sheets.

"Preston, undo my zipper, it's caught. I want to go to bed."

He slowly sat up and the sheets fell away from his bare chest. "Sit down on the bed. I'm not getting up," he grumbled. He smelled strongly of mouthwash and toothpaste.

She perched on the edge of the bed. "Lean over," he ordered, pushing her neck down. He began struggling with the zipper. Lacey could feel his breath brushing the bare portion of her back. After much cursing on his part, and patience on hers, he unzipped the dress to the top of her lavender silk panties, which was the only other thing she had on.

His finger went softly up to the nape of her neck, and trailed slowly down her spine. She was afraid to move, afraid he'd stop. She had to hold the strapless dress up over her breasts, but when she felt his hand snake beneath the material and work its way to the front, she gladly let the dress fall away. Looking down she could see his dark hand cupping her soft white breast, and her brain shut down completely. She no longer cared if he was frustrating. She only knew this felt good, very good.

Suddenly his hand stopped, and he pulled away, and fell back against his pillow.

"Lacey, you better go," he whispered.

Bitterly disappointed, she pulled the dress up to cover her breasts, and walked slowly back to her room without looking at him. She slid out of the dress and hung it on the padded hanger and covered it with the clear plastic garment bag Cynthia had brought it over in. After washing out the stockings, she draped them over the shower pole, and climbed wearily into bed.

Preston lay still, willing himself not to be sick again and cursing himself for having such lousy timing. Lacey hadn't seemed to mind where they had been heading and he knew he hadn't. Damn. His stomach roiled and he groaned. Maybe this was for the best. He should be concentrating on winning the race. A wave of nausea hit him again, and he sprinted to the bathroom.

The sun woke her up again, or maybe it was her stomach growling. She realized that she had eaten very little the night before, so, after seeing Preston's door was still closed, she showered and hurried over to the clubhouse breakfast buffet. She took her plate piled with waffles, and a large portion of fresh fruit to a small table outside in the sunshine, overlooking the ocean. Several couples were milling about, but none stopped by her table to speak to her. She was glad when Henry joined her with the news that Rodney was having all his meals via room service, and rumor had it that she was the reason. Everyone had heard about her pushing him off the dock.

After she finished eating, Henry suggested they ramble around the massive gardens in the compound. Lacey was glad of any excuse to avoid Preston.

"You know, Preston has changed, Lacey." Henry interrupted her pleasure in drinking in the myriad of riotous color in the flower garden.

"What do you mean?" She turned her head away so Henry couldn't tell how interested she was in what he was about to say.

Henry grinned at her obvious interest. "His father played a cruel trick on everyone. Not only did he leave Preston and his mother in financial limbo, but he also left many clients with bad investments and huge losses. Most of the yacht club members were Rockwell clients. Money is a very important part of Palm Beach social life. Most men would rather lose their wives than their money."

"So what are you saying, exactly?" she asked curiously.

"I'm saying that a lesser man would have quit the yacht club rather than brazen out this race. A lesser man would have cut his losses and moved on to new territory. I didn't think Preston could handle the pressure, but he's doing it. I think of all the people surprised by Preston, he's the most surprised of all."

She wondered what this had to do with her.

"My advice is to hang in there with Preston. He needs someone like you, Lacey. He just doesn't realize it yet," said Henry.

She turned away, embarrassed. "It shows," she whispered.

Henry reached over and hugged her. "Don't worry, I like the stupid idiot too. I'll walk you back to the cottage."

After a friendly good-bye, Lacey entered the cottage and gathered all the clean linens and headed for the boat. Preston's door was still shut, and she decided to let him sleep.

On board, she was amazed at how many supplies had appeared. Henry had been very thorough. Even the head was stocked with washcloths, bath towels, toilet paper, razors, a small mirror, and shaving cream. She dragged both bunk mattresses out of the narrow companionway and lay them flat on deck to air in the sun.

After borrowing a broom from a neighboring boat, she swept out the cabin, disgusted at the debris she gathered. She took the glass cleaner she found under the galley sink, and vigorously cleaned every item of glass she could find on the boat, paying special attention to the portholes and hatch. The navy blue curtains hanging over the portholes were stiff and crusty, so she removed them to wash when she returned to the cottage. Someone jumped on board, and she went up the steps with her hand shading her eyes to see who it was.

"Oh, it's you." She dropped her hand and attempted to turn over one of the mattresses. Preston reached down to help her. When both mattresses were turned over and airing to her satisfaction, he rubbed the back of his neck with his hand.

"I'm sorry about last night."

"Which part?" She began beating the mattresses with the broom. Clouds of dust puffed up and she sneezed. Preston stopped the broom in mid-air with one hand.

"All of it."

Lacey pulled the broom away from him and leaned on it. "The part where you ruined the only dress-up affair I have ever attended? Or the part where you told me that you wished Cynthia was your partner rather than me because she's such a good sailor?" Preston winced. He didn't remember saying that, but the venom in her voice was a clear indication he had. "Or the part where you began feeling me up, but then threw me out of your room? Which part exactly are you sorry for, Preston?"

"Everything except the feeling you up part. I—"

She picked up the broom and swung it angrily. Preston ducked, but she hit the mattress instead of him. "I'm sick of being with you," she said, continuing to beat the ever-loving hell out of the mattresses. "If you want Cynthia and me to trade places, I'll sail back with Rodney. I checked the rule book, and as along as the race committee agrees, it's legal." She turned back to whomp the mattresses and to hide her face from him.

"I don't want Cynthia for a partner any more, and from what I hear, Rodney doesn't want you. Lacey, that was alcohol on an empty stomach talking stupid last night. I really want you as my partner."

"My mom always told me that a person's true self emerges when they are inebriated."

Preston took her by the shoulders and turned her around. "Listen to me, Lacey. I'd rather have you as my partner, even if I lose." He hadn't expected to mean it when he said it, but he found to his amazement that he did.

* * *

Somewhat mollified by Preston's reassurance, Lacey hurried back to the cottage and began packing. Since they were setting sail in the dead of night, she left out a pair of jeans, and a sweatshirt. Everything but her toothbrush, she packed up and lugged down to the *Stud Muffin*.

She felt better than she had for days, comfortable in the familiar surroundings of the cabin. She filled her locker with her clean clothes, and sneaked a peek into Preston's to find it stuffed with clothes. The galley now had dish detergent, dish cloths, and dish towels, plus an array of cans and jars she knew she'd enjoy organizing later. She was anxious to set sail, but she could tell by the position of the sun, they had about fourteen more hours on land.

She returned to the cottage and was relieved to find Preston poring over the maps and charts on the kitchen table. She stood over him and looked down, liking the way the nape of his neck looked, bent over in study.

"Where are we now?"

He pointed to a tiny bay on the island. "Our problem will be sailing against the Gulf Stream. It's a cinch the wind won't be with us going back."

"Will we still sail in shifts?"

"Yes, but maybe shorter ones. I'll have to show you in daylight how to go against the wind tomorrow, and I'll take tonight's shift." He folded the charts back.

"We need to get some rest this afternoon." He grinned up at her. "For some reason I don't think we got much sleep last night, and I'm bushed."

Lacey smiled back. "I'm bushed, too."

She picked up the phone. "I'll put in a wake-up call for five and we can both take a nap."

He stretched lazily. "Good. Then we'll eat, and go on down to the boat and watch everyone leave until it's our turn."

While Lacey was on the phone with the compound operator, Preston went into his bedroom and lay on top of the covers. She hung up and hesitated briefly at his door before going into her bedroom. It took her over an hour of tossing and turning to get to sleep.

The sun was low in the sky when the revelers and contestants began gathering on the pier for what appeared to be yet another party. Bottles of champagne were passed from person to person, and the clubhouse provided tables of hors d'oeuvres near the entrance of the dock. Preston kept his head down and pushed his way through the crowd at a pace Lacey couldn't possibly keep up with, especially since many of her previous night's dance partners stopped to speak to her.

When she finally reached the boat, Preston was glowering at her from the seat at the helm.

"Are you sure my absence ruined your evening last night?" he asked sarcastically.

Lacey ignored him and went down into the cabin. He couldn't quit starting arguments with her, and she wasn't about to be pulled into another round of verbal warfare. She stood next to her bunk for a few minutes and returned on deck, determined to ignore Preston and his comments.

Everyone was laughing and chatting, strolling from

boat to boat, arm in arm, as if they hadn't a care in the world. Lacey envied them all their carefree attitude. Preston was facing towards the bay as if to discourage anyone from boarding, though it didn't stop Henry and his father, the plump man who had met them when they had docked almost forty-eight hours ago, from jumping on deck.

"Hey, Preston!"

Preston turned his head slowly around and grinned when he saw it was Henry. He jumped up and came over with his hand extended.

"Henry, Mr. Reese." He beamed at them and shook their hands. "Thank you for all you've done. You've both been lifesavers to me these past few months."

Henry's father laughed. "Pres, you know you'd have done the same thing for us. Don't make a big deal out of it."

Henry pulled a paper bag from behind his back and handed it to Lacey. "I got you a souvenir of Bermuda."

Lacey looked at the bag in surprise and took it from him. "Oh, Henry. You didn't have to get me anything." She could swear Henry's face was turning red.

"It's not that much, but I thought of you when I saw it."

Lacey tore open the bag and held up a yellow T-shirt with 'Bermuda' embroidered on the front in a rainbow of colors. "Henry, it's beautiful." She reached up and kissed him on the cheek, and there was no mistaking his blush this time. "I'm going to put it on." She raced down below to change shirts, but not before noticing Preston's sour look.

When she returned, Henry's father was climbing onto the dock, and Henry was standing awkwardly, awaiting his turn to disembark. She twirled in front of him and gave him a quick hug, when she noticed he was staring uncomfortably over her shoulder at Preston.

"See you in Palm Beach," mumbled Henry, as he walked rapidly up the pier.

Lacey turned on Preston. "What did you say to him?" she demanded.

"Nothing," came his sullen answer.

"Preston Rockwell, your friend was being kind to me, and he's been wonderful to you. If I find out you hurt his feelings . . ." The threat trailed off.

"I wasn't aware Henry meant so much to you."

"If you are going to revert back to a pig-headed child again, I swear I'll, oh, I don't know." She stamped her foot in frustration. "You do this every time, Preston. You tear down a wall between us, only to build it right back up. What are you afraid of?"

Preston looked out towards the bay, and Lacey let loose an exasperated expletive before climbing up onto the dock and threading her way through the crowd to the table of goodies. She had no appetite, but anything was better than sharing the deck with a sulking Preston.

She bumped into Rodney, of all people, at the table. He gave her a look of pure hatred, before turning abruptly and walking away into the crowd. Cynthia sidled up beside her. "Mr. Fleming is in quite a temper. I'm going to have a pleasant ride home."

"I guess I shouldn't have pushed him off the dock, but I couldn't stop myself."

"I've almost pushed him overboard twice, getting

here. The man's a beast and a menace, but he can sail. See you in Palm Beach." She disappeared into the crowd.

Lacey put one shrimp, one crab-stuffed mushroom, and one cracker spread with what she assumed was caviar on her china plate. She would have served food in paper plates and paper cups, not china and crystal, especially outside. Someone came up behind her, and she sensed it was Preston, so she resisted the impulse to turn around.

"Lacey . . ." Preston said, grabbing her hand and dragging her through the crowds to the *Stud Muffin*. She had a difficult time keeping her food from sliding off her plate. When they reached the deck, he turned to her.

"Lacey, listen," he said so seriously, her heart almost stopped.

"I'm tremendously attracted to you, but my first priority is winning this race. I have to win to get enough money to save my mother's estate for her. Do you understand? That's why I can't give you more money if we win. I need almost every penny."

"What if we lose?"

"If we lose, Lacey, I can't even pay you the twenty-five hundred. I'm broke. Flat broke." He watched her face closely, gauging her reaction.

"Oh, Preston." Her shoulders slumped as she leaned against the mast.

"I should have told you sooner. I'm sorry."

"I know I should be angrier than hell at you, but I'm not. I needed the money for selfish reasons— nothing noble."

"Do you understand how this race has to be my number one priority?"

"As opposed to your attraction to me?" she asked, her eyes wide and innocent.

"Well, yes." Preston looked away. "This just isn't a good time for me to become involved with someone."

"Me either. Maybe it's just our constant proximity to each other on this boat."

"Yeah. That's probably it."

"And sex would ruin our friendship and I don't want that, Preston. I kind of like you sometimes, when you're not being a complete jerk."

He grinned. "That much, huh?"

She grinned back. "You've actually been pleasant to be around about a total of four hours."

"Very funny. Anyway, the *Filthy Rich* should be setting sail soon. She was the first boat in."

"So all we can do is wait."

"Correct." He went below, feeling somewhat deflated, and left Lacey on deck.

Well, Preston had certainly set things straight. She picked up her plate and slowly ate her shrimp and mushroom. Why was he coming clean now? Was it an indication that he cared for her, as well as being attracted? She didn't mind that he was broke. Somehow, it brought him within her reach. Oh well, she'd have days to analyze her feelings, and observe him closely. She bit into the caviar and promptly ran to spit it overboard. Yeck! If that's what rich people liked to snack on, she was glad she had no money. Give her plain old peanut butter on a cracker, any day.

Ten

Preston tried to ignore the hoopla when the other ships had set sail earlier in the night, but it had sounded like a marina-wide Mardi Gras outside, and he hadn't been able to sleep a wink, even with his pillow wedged over his head. When things finally settled down, a little after midnight, he went up on deck, only to find Lacey missing. He glanced at his watch and wondered where in the world she could have gone.

Most of the revelers had apparently left after seeing off the next-to-the-last contestant, and the dock looked fairly empty except for the three yawning judges sitting outside the building at the end of the dock. He walked up the pier towards shore, and saw Lacey in the shadows, sitting on the dock with her knees clasped to her chest. She was gesturing wildly to someone who sat too far into the darkness for Preston to identity.

He began walking rapidly towards them and was relieved to recognize Henry sitting cross-legged near her. Between them lay the large platter of shrimp from the table.

Lacey looked sheepishly up at him. "Hi. I got hungry, and Henry was nice enough to keep me company while I cleaned off this platter."

Preston hunched down next to them and picked up a shrimp. "We've still got another forty minutes before we can leave. I hate waiting."

"You still have the lead, Preston. I think you may win this one," Henry said encouragingly.

Preston popped the shrimp into his mouth and stood up.

"Do you think we should get back to the boat?" asked Lacey.

"Just be there by twelve forty-five, at least." He started down the pier.

Lacey watched Preston walk away and looked over at Henry. "Maybe I should go now." She stood up and dusted off her jeans. Henry got up and walked with her down the pier.

"I'll ask around Palm Beach about restaurant jobs for you, if you're sure that's what you want."

"It's what I know and love, Henry. And if we lose, I'll be destitute. He told me tonight he couldn't even pay me the twenty-five hundred we agreed upon. That's okay, though. I like working." She nudged him in the ribs with her elbow. "You should try it sometime."

Henry laughed. "Not until I have to. For some reason, work has never appealed to me." He watched her climb onto the boat. "Take care, Lacey. And be patient."

Lacey wrinkled her nose. "That's my middle name. See ya in Palm Beach."

Henry yawned. "I'd stay and see you two off, but I'm bushed. Bye." He gave a little wave, and disappeared into the night.

"Do you like Henry?" Preston's voice came from the darkness behind her.

"Oh, gosh. You startled me." Lacey held her hand to her chest.

"You didn't answer the question."

"Yes, I do, very much," she answered truthfully.

"What did he mean by 'be patient?' "

"Preston, exactly where is this line of questioning leading?"

He reached up to rub the back of his neck with his hand. "I don't know. Forget it."

"If you must know, I asked him to look for a job for me in Palm Beach." She carefully studied his features in the half light.

"You're thinking of staying in Palm Beach?" Preston had brightened considerably.

Her own mood lightened at his tone. He sounded, well, happy. "Yes. I like it there. I'd like to be near water I can swim in. Seattle is too cold."

"Great." He gave her a huge smile. "If anyone can find you a job, Henry can. Let's go ahead and get the mainsail up."

The judges came over and grudgingly watched Preston and Lacey set sail exactly forty-eight hours after they had docked in Bermuda. An hour later they left the shelter of the bay, and were relieved to find a steady wind, though the current against them was stronger than expected. Preston raised the mizzen as they entered the ocean, and the *Stud Muffin* picked up speed.

"Where do you think the others might be?" she asked, squinting into the horizon.

Preston glanced at his watch. "They all probably passed St. David's Head lighthouse by now and are just heading southwest. I'd say we have an hour or more advantage on the *Filthy Rich*."

Lacey helped Preston get everything set, before going below for some needed rest. Staying in Bermuda had been more tiring than the sailing so far.

Lacey awoke with a start when the boat pitched suddenly. If she hadn't been tucked snugly into the bedding of the bunk, she would have been thrown onto the floor. She pulled on her shorts and raced out on deck, almost sliding on the water-soaked wood.

"What happened?" she yelled, blanching as a wall of water barreled towards them, only to violently tilt the boat and move away.

Preston was soaked. Water was dripping from his hair and nose. "I wasn't watching properly," he sputtered. "Go down and put on a life belt. It's rougher out here than it looks."

Lacey went below and hurriedly put on the flotation device. She could swim, but she wasn't sure how well in water this wild.

She worked her way over towards Preston, and he let her take the wheel, but stood behind her with his hands near hers on the smooth wood. "Okay, we need to cut into these waves at a 45-degree angle, but stay on course as much as possible. We're heading south-southwest. The current keeps pulling, so we won't be able to lash the helm any more." He helped her get the feel of the motion of the waves. There was a kind of rhythm that she soon picked up. After a hour of watching her, and when he saw she was fairly comfortable with the motion of the wheel, he moved away slightly.

"I think we better start shortening our watches to four hours on, four hours off."

Lacey looked back at him, and saw the strain in his face. "Okay. Be sure to get something to eat down there, too."

He looked impatiently at her. "If anything comes up you can't handle, or you are unsure of, call me. I'll leave the hatch open."

"Yes, I will," she promised. He disappeared down the companionway.

Lacey gripped the wheel with all her strength, and prayed she'd last the four hours of fighting current and wind. The life belt was uncomfortable, but she didn't dare remove it. The waves seemed larger by the minute. She hadn't realized how small the *Stud Muffin* was until now.

Preston toweled himself off and peeled off his wet jeans. His attention had only wandered a minute, and the wave had hit the *Stud Muffin* broadside. The mast had almost touched the water. He wasn't sure Lacey could handle these seas, but he needed the rest. Maybe he'd go up in three hours to relieve her. He curled up under the clean bedding and went promptly to sleep.

On Lacey's third watch, late in the afternoon, a storm began to develop. The clouds gathered on the horizon, until the sky turned dark and ominous. The sea and sky blended, and only the slashes of lightning cutting from the clouds to the water gave any indication where the ocean stopped, and the sky began. By now the waves were getting even larger, and the boat pitched to the side and seemed to take forever to right itself again.

No wonder Preston had kept saying that sailing wasn't all that easy. Her stomach churned, but she wasn't sure whether it was from seasickness or from anxiety. As the storm drew closer, she was torn between letting Preston rest, and waking him up to see if there was something she should be doing to prepare the *Stud Muffin* from the inevitable onslaught of the storm.

Finally, as the lightning slashed closer and closer, she lost her nerve and frantically called Preston. It was several minutes before he came up on deck, and by then Lacey was panicking.

He could almost smell her fear from the companionway. He rushed over and took the wheel from her.

"Preston, the lightning keeps hitting the water. Will we be safe in this boat?"

"I've sailed through storms before, Lacey. Better go below and bring me my foul weather gear. I think I'm going to need it." As she stumbled into the cabin, Preston tapped the barometer. It was falling rapidly and he squinted against the constant spray to see the sails flapping in the bursts of wind.

When Lacey brought him the yellow slicker, she also included a life belt. "Put it on. I can't afford to lose you." He managed a quick grin as he fastened the belt around his waist.

"I'm going to have to reef the sails."

She looked at him blankly.

He saw her look. "Tighten the sails so they don't flap so much," he explained. "Hold the wheel while I turn the boom and roll the mainsail tighter."

Lacey trembled as she held fast. The spray was

hammering at her fast and furious and she could barely open her eyes. Preston moved as quickly as possible, hanging on with one hand to the handrails mounted on the top of the cabin. Reefing usually took two people, but he didn't dare lash down the helm in this weather. As soon as the task was completed, he relieved Lacey. "Be sure you strap yourself to the galley wall and don't cook anything using grease. We're heading right into a squall and it's going to get worse before it gets better." Lacey's face went pale.

Preston continued. "I'm going to lash myself to the ring where we've been lashing the helm, and if you come out again, I want you to tie your life belt to some of the nylon rope and secure the cord to one of these handrails. The emergency dinghy is in the locker right inside the door if we need it. All you have to do is pull the cord and it inflates."

"Preston, I'm afraid of lightning."

He pointed to the top of the mast. "Lightning rod."

Great. They were advertising for lightning to strike and that was supposed to make her feel better. Lightning rods never had made sense to her. She went down into the cabin and secured the cabin door, opening the locker to assure herself that the emergency raft was indeed there.

Henry had told her to use the green spigot at the tiny sink to get gravity drawn saltwater to use for doing dishes, instead of wasting the precious fresh water. She cleaned up and as the pitching increased, she took to her bunk and willed her lunch to stay down.

When the rain hit, it hit full force. Preston could

barely see the compass. The wind increased several knots, but wasn't consistent in direction. No matter how hard he tried, he could no longer prevent an occasional wave from washing over the deck. Luckily, almost everything was still battened down from their days spent in Bermuda.

Lacey sat on her bunk, her eyes wide with fear. The single bulb had flickered out, and she was clutching the flashlight she had kept in the tiny hammock that swung over the foot of her bed. She could hear the waves slapping the sides of the cabin and the rain hitting the top hatch, but it wasn't until she aimed the light onto the floor and noticed almost an inch of water sloshing back and forth that she became frozen in fear.

"Lacey!"

Hesitating only a moment, she donned her foul weather gear and tied the line to her life belt before going outside. Preston was waiting to knot her nylon rope securely to the handrail. The storm was loud, and it took all her concentration to hear and understand Preston. "I'm going to drop anchor fore and aft so that we aren't blown too far off course. I'm not sure how deep the water is here, though, so we may have to try this a few times. Then we're going to pull down the sails and heave to. I'm afraid the wind is going to tear them up. Go hold onto the helm while I drop the anchors."

Lacey fought the wind and rain and barely kept her balance enough to reach the wheel. Each time the bow dipped into a wave and washed over the deck, she thought it was the end of the *Stud Muffin*. Preston had lashed himself by a longer length of rope to the handrail and was releasing the anchor chain with a large winch at the bow. He let almost all the chain out before he seemed satisfied. He made his way aft and after waiting for the boat to swing around, lowered a smaller anchor.

"You can let go of the wheel now," he shouted. "Come help me get down the sails."

He positioned Lacey under the mainsail. "Do what you have to do to keep this thing from floating away. I have some spare sails, but not a mainsail."

Lacey watched as he lowered the sail with lines and pulleys, and she ran over to bundle it in her arms as best she could. She had to wait for Preston to unroll and release the bottom of the sail from the boom, and together they dragged it down the companionway, along with a good portion of the ocean, and left it on the floor of the cabin. They repeated the process for all four sails. Preston lashed the boom so it wouldn't swing wildly and joined her in the now dark, damp cabin.

He pulled off his foul weather gear and threw it on the floor. "What now?" asked Lacey.

"I think I better work the bilge pump to get rid of some of the water." He lit a kerosene lamp fastened to the wall next to the galley, with a lighter that was tied to it, and another one near the head. "Then we're going to try and straighten out the sails, and wait out the storm."

"What's a bilge pump?" she asked, trying to follow Preston towards the front of the cabin.

He worked out a panel from the floor and dropped down. "Get a flashlight, will you?"

Lacey grabbed the flashlight and leveled it into the hole where Preston was standing. To her horror, he was standing in about two feet of water. "Are we sinking?" She tried to keep the hysteria out of her voice.

"No." He began working a metal handle, and in no time, she could see more and more of his legs in the murky water. After awhile, he lifted himself out of the hole and returned the panel. By the light of the two kerosene lanterns, they separated the sails into piles, and Preston checked them carefully for damage. They tried in vain to fold the wet polyester, but gave up. Preston sat on his haunches and looked at her. "There's nothing more we can do but ride out the storm."

Every part of Lacey's body hurt from being thrown against things. She couldn't understand how on earth this tiny boat was staying afloat. Preston stood up and began pulling off his wet clothes and throwing them in a pile near the head. He wrapped himself in a towel and stopped and looked at Lacey. Her eyes were clamped shut.

"Lacey, you better get out of your wet things, too. I won't look." He spoke as gently as possible over the roar of the squall.

Lacey stood up and went into the head to undress and wrap a towel around herself. Preston was pushing a towel tightly under the door to the deck to keep out some of the rain and ocean. He turned and crawled into his bunk. Lacey clung to her towel and anything else she could use to keep her balance as she made her precarious way to her bunk. She crawled awkwardly in and lay rigidly on her back, holding onto the sides as tightly as possible. Preston could see she was fighting for control.

"I've sailed in worse storms, Lacey. We'll be fine."

The boat pitched starboard and almost tossed Preston to the floor.

"Lacey?" No answer. "Lacey, are you all right?"

"No," she whispered. "I'm scared."

"Do you want me to come over there?" What possessed him to ask, he wasn't sure, but he held his breath waiting for her answer.

"Yes," came her faint reply through the rumble of the thunder.

He clasped the towel around his middle and crawled from his bunk to hers. She buried her head in his shoulder and wrapped her arms around him.

"Don't be scared. We'll be okay."

"I never get scared," she whispered. "Well, hardly ever."

"When were you last frightened?" Preston smoothed the damp curls from her face. Maybe if he kept her talking, she wouldn't notice the thunder, or the bright flashes of lightning that intermittently lit the cabin.

"Standing on the front porch of the house where my father lived, after I finally located him. It took me almost a year to track him down when I was eighteen. That was the most frightened I've ever been." She nuzzled closer.

"And why was that?" Preston asked as the boat pitched starboard again, pushing his weight against Lacey.

"He was so angry I had found him. He had a new wife and four kids, and he said he sure as hell didn't need me showing up. He told me to leave and never come back."

Preston heard the catch in her voice. "He sounds ignorant."

"Maybe there's something wrong with me or something."

"Why would you say that?" He put his thumb under her chin and made her lift her eyes to his. Even in the poor light of the lanterns, he could see her eyes were swimming in tears.

"My own father didn't want me. Frank didn't want . . ." her voice trailed off.

"Who's Frank?" Preston felt a pang of some emotion he had never felt before.

"A guy I was engaged to in Seattle." She lowered her head.

"What happened?"

Lacey buried her face into his neck.

"Well?"

"He called off the wedding."

Wedding. Lacey had once planned a wedding, a life with someone. And she obviously still had feelings for the guy.

"Why?"

"He met someone better—my stepsister." She couldn't keep the bitterness out of her voice, nor the pain.

"Ouch," said Preston.

"Yeah, ouch. It wouldn't have been so bad if he'd dumped me for a stranger, but I have to see them together at every family event. It's horrible."

"I meant ouch, my back is pressing into the edge of the bunk."

Lacey scooted closer to the outside wall of the cabin, and Preston slid closer to her and tightened his arms around her. "They are both jerks, Lacey. It's good that they don't want you, because you deserve better people in your life anyway. They probably knew that."

"Sure," she agreed sarcastically.

"I mean it. You don't need people that don't appreciate you. You're smart and pretty. You're not like any woman I've ever known. You're special."

She raised up on one elbow and looked down at him. "Thank you. That's the nicest thing anyone other than my mother has ever said to me."

"I'm not just saying it. You've helped me tremendously on this trip. You stayed outside in weather that frightened you, and helped me do what had to be done. You've put up with my mood swings, ignored my abominable behavior, and then were kind enough to take care of me when I needed it. You're wonderful."

Lacey forgot the wind, the storm, the high seas. She lay back on her pillow and pulled Preston closer to her. He lifted his head to gently brush her lips. "I wish we had met after the race. I wish this race wasn't so damn important to me. I wish . . ."

Lacey pulled his face back down to hers and kissed him on the lips. "Shut up."

Preston ran his hands up into her hair and turned her head ever so slightly, kissing her repeatedly about the face. The next time he kissed her lips, he carefully explored her mouth with his tongue.

Lacey felt his hot hardness pressed against her thigh. Their towels had somehow worked their way from their bodies, and his skin was smooth and warm against hers. Her hands twined into his hair and down around his neck. Their breathing was audible over the whistling gale force winds. He worked his hand under the blanket and touched her breast. It hadn't been a dream the other night, after all. He moved aside the blanket and looked down at the pale pink nipple budding beneath his fingers. With a groan he lowered his head and kissed her breasts. When he raised his head, she was looking down at him.

"Are you sure?" he asked, his voice rough with desire.

She nodded, wanting nothing more than to ease the mounting excitement growing within her. She pulled his face back up to hers and caressed his back as his fingers feathered over her breasts. His hand lowered past the flat of her stomach, just as hers tentatively traveled the line of hair growing down from his navel.

Together they stroked each other in the most intimate fashion, Preston surprised at how ready she was for him, and Lacey awed by his pulsating splendor. He lifted himself over her and looked down at her half-closed eyes. She spread her legs and guided him inside herself. They gasped in unison and smiled at each other. Preston lowered himself until he was sheathed in her wet softness and he kissed her long and deep as he moved in a rhythm that matched the pitching of the boat.

Lacey wrapped her legs around Preston's hips and they moved together, Lacey finding a rhythm of her own that began a slow, deep burning growing inside. Preston arched himself over her at the moment of his climax and seconds later, she too arched repeatedly and sighed with pure pleasure. They lay limply together, too weak to move. Preston finally raised his head and kissed both her eye lids. "You're wonderful."

He rolled off her and bundled her tightly against him. She turned on her side and snuggled her backside against the curve of his hips, her back against the flat of his stomach. She pulled his arm over her and held it tightly against her chest. He smiled to himself at how quickly she had forgotten the lightning and thunder. They both closed their eyes and fell into a deep, dreamless sleep, oblivious to the storm outside.

Eleven

When Lacey awoke, she felt a throbbing between her legs which made her blush. Preston had disappeared and she dreaded the awkward, uncomfortable confrontation which was sure to come. The ship was rolling less than the previous day and she could hear no rain beating against the hatch. After hesitating a few minutes, she hurriedly dressed, put on her life belt, took a deep breath, and went up on deck.

The waves were huge swells with the slightest whitecaps on top. Their massive size dwarfed the *Stud Muffin,* but amazingly, they didn't break over the deck, just rolled the boat unmercifully. Preston was winching up the aft anchor, sweat pouring from his brow. Every so often he would stop, curse, and wipe the sweat from out of his eyes.

She stumbled below and removed her life belt. Though the stove was not gimbaled, the rolling motion was side to side, and the worse anything could spill was into the sink, not onto her. She started a saucepan of water boiling for coffee and wished now she hadn't bought decaffeinated. Someone had added six eggs to the ice chest, so she popped four in to boil in the other saucepan. Like it or not, he was going to eat.

She toasted two pieces of bread on the other

burner and peeled the eggs. She was preparing to go get Preston, when he lumbered into the cabin, splattering water everywhere.

"The anchor is snagged on something. We'll have to try and sail behind it and free it up from a different angle."

"Good morning," she mumbled under her breath.

"Let's get the mainsail up. The wind is blowing at least forty knots, so we should be able to work up some power."

"Can we eat breakfast first? Or maybe have a cup of coffee?"

"Have you forgotten this is a race? We can eat later." He picked up the mainsail and began dragging it up the companionway.

Lacey turned off the burners with a snap and put on her foul weather gear and life belt. So much for romance, sentiment, and awkward confrontations. She helped push the last of the sail up the companionway, and sat on it to keep it from blowing into the sea while Preston fastened all the rigging.

"Okay, now hold it here and let out a little at a time as I hoist it." He pulled on the hanging lines and Lacey fed out small lengths of sail, keeping it from fouling or twisting around the boom. When it was hoisted all the way, it billowed and grew taut in the wind. Preston worked his way to the helm. "Come here," he yelled. "Hold this steady. We're going to sail backwards over the anchor, and I'm going to try and winch it up."

The boat slid easily over the chain and she could feel a sudden jerk when the full length of chain went taut. Preston pulled and huffed behind her, letting out a string of curses that raised her eyebrows. He finally stood, and disappeared below. When he returned, he was wielding a large pair of bolt cutters. He hacked at one of the chain links until one side cut through. In no time, the pull of the boat had stretched the cut link until it snapped and the boat started sailing top speed with a jerk.

Preston turned the boom so that the mainsail could take full advantage of the wind. "What direction are we going?" he yelled.

"Southwest," she shouted back. He nodded his head in satisfaction.

She watched as he dragged out the back sail and painstakingly rigged it, despite the wind and water. A wave broke over the bow, and Preston had to scramble to grab one of the smaller sails before it washed overboard.

"Go into the waves at an angle, not straight on!"

"I'm sorry." Lacey gripped the wheel even harder, and wondered how she was supposed to tell one wave from another. There was an army of waves marching towards the *Stud Muffin,* and at the speed they were traveling, she could do little more than point the boat in the general direction she wanted to go.

He continued raising sails, and how he ever accomplished it in the condition he was in, and alone at that, she'd never know. She could tell he was exhausted when he came over to relieve her.

"Go on down and eat your breakfast, and then I need to rest up some. The barometer isn't going up, so we could hit more weather."

Lacey stumbled below and swallowed her eggs and toast almost whole, suddenly ravenous. She didn't drink any coffee, afraid she'd have to go to the head later. As quickly as she could, she raced back on deck.

Preston looked relieved to see her, but didn't speak as he disappeared below. Last night might have never happened, she thought.

Preston wished last night *had* never happened. He removed his foul weather gear and stood panting in the galley. He had dreaded seeing Lacey this morning. The hard work and busyness had been welcome, as he was able to avoid almost all contact. He, Preston Rockwell, was frightened of how this petite redhead made him feel. He had nothing to offer her. He wasn't worthy of Lacey Campbell.

They exchanged watch every four hours until dusk, when Preston insisted Lacey go below as she was far too inexperienced to sail at night. The wind and waves had not let up, and a fine mist began to fall from the overcast skies. When on deck, they both now automatically donned the bright yellow rain gear and orange life belts, though they had ceased lashing themselves to the deck. The deck chair had been washed overboard the day before and they had to sit on a flotation cushion they found in one of the storage closets.

Every time Preston took over for Lacey, he found they were off course by a few miles. He knew she was doing her best, so he kept the knowledge to himself. He figured that they had lost up to four hours adjusting their position on course after each of her watches.

Lacey took Preston a mugful of soup. She didn't bother to don her gear or belt.

"Don't come out here again without dressing for it," he growled from under his rain hood.

Lacey didn't answer. She had difficulty keeping her balance in the poor light. She cleaned up the galley and decided Preston could throw the mug overboard before she'd go up and get it from him. She pulled off her wet clothes and climbed gratefully into the bunk. She could still smell the slight scent of Preston's shampoo on her pillow. She slammed it with her fist and flipped it over. How could she have been so stupid?

At dawn, Preston shouted until she heard him. She rushed on deck with the blanket wrapped around her to meet his baleful stare. "Get your stuff on before you take watch."

"I thought there was an emergency," she said indignantly. She rubbed her eyes and pulled on her last pair of dry jeans and a sweat shirt, before donning the required gear. She slipped onto deck and took her position behind the wheel. Preston turned his back and slowly worked his way below, his legs stiff from sitting in the damp. He wondered how far off course they would be next time he came out.

Lacey tried in vain to keep the compass pointing south, but each wave was against her. Twice the waves had broken over the deck, causing her to cling to the wheel for dear life. The rain was still light, but the heavy rubber hood made it hard to see anywhere but straight ahead. She thought she caught a glimpse of another ship nearby a few times, but the waves made it difficult to see any distance. She concentrated on the compass.

Two hours later, she was sure there was another ship approaching. When riding on the crest of a wave, she could see a mast not all that far away. She debated whether or not to call Preston, but since there was little he could do but get even grumpier, she decided not to. The ship was coming fast over the waves, almost as if it were surfing rather than sailing. She became alarmed when she decided that maybe the other ship couldn't see them and they might be on a crash course. She screamed for Preston. He finally emerged in full gear, just as a huge wave washed over the boat, taking Preston with it.

The other ship was upon them and she immediately sounded the fog horn in an SOS signal. It was the *Filthy Rich,* so close she could read the name, and though Rodney was visible on deck, he kept his head turned resolutely away from Lacey's hysterical waving. Cynthia was not in sight.

She had to save Preston. She closed her eyes and remembered he had on his life belt and bright yellow gear, so she might be able to spot him. She turned the helm in the direction of the waves and headed back, the boom groaning from the sudden change of direction. The wind caught in the sails and began pushing her backwards.

Sobbing, she lashed the helm and lowered the mainsail as she had seen Preston do. It flapped and drooped, some of it sliding overboard. She wished she knew about auxiliary engines, but she didn't. The waves pushed her back in the direction they had come from, and she scanned the water with the binoculars, constantly wiping the lenses dry with her sweatshirt. She spotted a yellow flash on the horizon and began turning the boat starboard.

Her heart in her throat, the boat seemed to take forever to get near the yellow object, which kept disappearing behind the huge waves. Only when she saw what appeared to be a head and two arms, did her heart lift. She ran and lowered two more of the sails, leaving them to puddle on deck. She was afraid the *Stud Muffin* would pass Preston before she could throw the life preserver over.

When Preston's face came into view, she could see he was terrified. That made two of them. She flung over the life preserver, and held her breath waiting to see if he had managed to grab hold. She looked back and saw his head bobbing behind the boat as he pulled himself in with the rope. She tried to pull the rope in herself, but couldn't. He finally grabbed onto some of the still-rigged sail that was dragging in the water and climbed aboard.

"I . . . I can't believe you did . . . did that," he sputtered between deep breaths.

"Me either." She rested her face in her shaking hands, oblivious to the roll of the boat. Her whole body was trembling with fear. She looked up, her face wet. "If you hadn't had on the yellow gear . . ."

Preston lay exhausted on the sails. "But I did. Why didn't that bastard stop? Could you see who it was?"

"It was Rodney."

"I heard the horn. Why didn't he?"

"He didn't want to hear it. He wouldn't even look over here. I hate him," she ground out between clenched teeth.

"The best way get back at him would be to win."

They looked at one another and in unison began pulling up sails. "We'll check for damage later. We need to get moving. I'll run down and change and you get us headed in the right direction."

When Preston emerged minutes later in fresh gear, Lacey was beaming from the helm. "The barometer is rising!"

Preston took over and sent her below. They were miles off course, but nothing that couldn't be fixed. Lacey fell into her bunk and slept soundly, still not believing how well she had kept her head in the crisis.

Lacey slept over ten hours. Preston was preparing to call her when she finally emerged from the cabin, blinking her eyes at the bright sunlight.

"Sorry," she apologized as she took over the helm. "I don't know why I'm so tired." She recalled what she had said and blushed. "When did the sun come out?"

"Not long after our incident." He stood out of her way and paused. "Do you think Rodney knew we were in trouble?"

Lacey gripped the wheel. "Yes, he knew all right. I could read the name of his boat, we were so close. He had to have heard the horn."

"Where was Cynthia?"

She turned to him. "I honestly didn't see her at all. Why?"

"Because Cynthia is an experienced racer who sticks strictly to the rules. She wouldn't have passed up a distress signal."

"Well, Preston, she did. They never came back to help."

Preston rubbed the back of his neck. "Oh well, I'm only going to take a quick nap. Watch the compass and head due south at all times."

"Okay." He watched a minute before heading below.

The wind was still blowing up nicely, but the waves were much friendlier looking than they had been, and much further apart. All the clouds were gone, and the sun was a bright ball heading for the west. She looked for the blue tarp, but found only a few pieces of plastic where it had been installed. The storm had claimed it too, she guessed. She shifted her feet and decided she sorely missed the chair they had used. It was going to be a long watch.

Preston stripped off his gear and sat on his bunk. He was still shaken over the morning's incident, though he hadn't given himself time to think about it all day. It was the closest he had ever come to death and his twenty minutes in the rolling ocean had given him plenty of time to think. Lacey had surprised him again. She'd turned the boat and found him. He lay back and put his arms under his head. She was full of surprises.

Later, when Lacey had fixed them a much-deserved meal, they leaned against the sides of the cockpit, their legs touching.

"That was great. I'm feeling better now." Preston rubbed his stomach with satisfaction.

"It was a hairy few days," Lacey said, leaning her head back and closing her eyes.

"How on earth did you manage to find me and bring the boat around?"

"I had to find you, Preston." Her eyes opened and she looked at him. "No way was I leaving you."

"Why? So I could sail the boat?" he asked curiously.

"No." She closed her eyes again and lay back.

Preston looked at her chin tilted in the air, and decided not to ask why she had been so determined to save him. A seed of hope began to germinate. "You still haven't explained how you knew what to do."

"My book," she answered lazily.

"Impossible," he said, shaking his head.

After a few minutes of silence, Lacey worked up her courage.

"Preston, about the other night . . ."

Preston's eyes remained closed. "What about it?"

She gnawed her bottom lip in vexation. "I don't usually do that."

"Do what?" He didn't move.

"You know! Jump into bed with just anyone," she said in frustration.

He opened his eyes and looked at her. "I was hoping I wasn't just anyone."

Lacey blushed. "Well, you're not. I didn't want you to think that."

"It never crossed my mind. You're not just anyone to me, either. But do you realize how broke I am?"

"What does that have to do with anything?" she frowned.

"I mean, I have absolutely nothing to offer you, unless I win the race. I know you want money . . ."

Lacey's face turned an alarming shade of red. "Preston Rockwell, I only wanted enough money to tide me over until I got a job. But if we won, I planned to use the money to help open my own restaurant. I don't want chauffeurs or limos or nannies or evening gowns. My dreams are pretty ordinary."

"Lacey, I don't even have a job."

"I thought you worked at an office with your father."

"I never really worked a day in my life. I used my

law degree to do routine title searches, or draw up papers and contracts. He just wanted my name engraved on the door. I don't even know what he did, really, besides gamble."

"You've got a law degree, but never had a job?" Lacey asked in amazement.

It was Preston's turn to be uncomfortable. "Well, I went to work each day, but I never lived paycheck to paycheck. However, if I lose this race, that's something I'll have to learn," he answered grimly. "Is there a *How To Be Broke* book?

Lacey grinned. "It's not all that bad, Preston."

He grinned back. "I'd rather win the race."

"I want to win, too, but now it's not the money. I refuse to let that heartless egomaniac Rodney Fleming win."

"Well, then let's beat the bastard. We'll keep the four hour watches."

"No, you sleep the rest of the afternoon, and sail tonight. I don't trust myself at night."

"You mean sailing?" he asked, grinning.

She gave him a withering look. "Yes, sailing. The weather is returning to normal, and I know I can keep us on course."

Preston hesitated, remembering all the corrective sailing he had to do in the last few days.

"It was the waves messing me up before. I promise I'll stay on course, and besides, I have my book."

Preston laughed. "Okay, but wake me around five. I want to see if I can get that radio to work long enough to call the Coast Guard."

"Aye, aye, Captain. Let me run down and get my sunglasses."

He watched her lunge below and smiled. Lacey didn't care but his money situation, or the scandal, or anything. She really was priceless.

Twelve

After Preston took over his shift, Lacey went below and made a pot of meatless spaghetti. As she worked, she found herself humming, and attributed it to the fact that Preston had lost that tense, pinched look, and was much more fun to be around. They ate in companionable silence.

After cleaning up the dishes, Lacey washed her hair, and went up on deck to let it dry in the wind. Preston was comfortably leaning against the back of the cockpit. She sat facing him, her legs crossed, and bent her head down and rubbed her hair vigorously with a towel.

"Look dead ahead." Preston nodded his head forward.

Lacey stopped, looked into the dark horizon and saw running lights far into the distance.

"Do you think it's the *Filthy Rich*?"

"It has to be. We should catch up, I would think, at least before we dock in Palm Beach."

"Can't we go any faster?"

Preston shook his head. "This is as fast as we get."

She looked back at Preston. "Do you really think we have a chance?"

"Yes. We should spot land late tomorrow, and I

figure we should pass the *Filthy Rich* sometime close to that."

Lacey combed her hair back with her fingers. "We deserve to win, Preston."

"I know. What's funny is that no one really needs the money, but me. The winner usually donates the purse to some charity. Fleming knows how badly I need the money."

"I shouldn't have pushed him off the pier," Lacey moaned.

"No way. That's the best thing you've done." He grinned. "I'll have that picture in my head to carry with me for the rest of my life, no matter what."

"But I think he wants to beat us now to salve his pride." Lacey frowned.

"No, he's just a mean bastard, and winning will hurt us both, and he knows it."

Lacey wrapped her arms around herself.

"Chilly?" Preston asked.

"Yeah. I guess I should go below and get some sleep."

"Come here and sit with me a little while." Preston held up his arm and motioned her to come sit next to him.

She smiled, and slid under his arm, resting her head on his shoulder. He slowly rubbed her arm and pulled her as close as possible.

"In two days, this will all be over."

"All?" Lacey asked impishly.

"The race part. After the race, we'll discuss us, I promise."

Lacey closed her eyes. It didn't seem fair that her future depended on a race. If they won, no problem, but if they lost, she knew his pride would ruin their budding relationship.

Preston knew exactly the minute when she fell asleep. Her body relaxed and her breathing slowed. What was he going to do about Lacey Campbell? No way was he going to ask her to join him in a life of struggle and poverty. Even if he landed a job with the most prestigious law firm in the country, it would be years before he could pay off the note on his mother's home. He looked down at her face. She looked like a child when she was asleep, and her delicate snore made him grin. He couldn't, he wouldn't hurt her, no matter what.

After twenty or so minutes, his arm began to go to sleep, and as much as he hated to disturb her, he really had no choice. "Lacey." He brushed her ear with his lips. "Lacey."

She stirred and he watched her eyes flutter open. She sat up, stretched and yawned. "I'm sorry. I better get in my bunk. I didn't realize I was so tired."

He stood up and pulled her to her feet. Giving her a quick hug, and a soft swat on the behind, he sent her below to sleep.

Try as he might, Preston could not get much closer to the boat ahead of them. He nervously watched the compass and barometer, wondering what he could do to pass the *Filthy Rich*. In frustration, he finally settled behind the wheel and stared dismally at the distant lights. What was he going to do if they lost? Tell his mother she no longer had a place to live? Ask Lacey to wait for him while he searched for a career, a home for his mother, a life? He couldn't ask that of her. They had to win.

* * *

"Look, we're gaining on them," Preston said when she came out on deck the next morning. Sure enough, they were close enough that she could read the *Filthy Rich* engraved on the back of Rodney's boat in gold leaf. She also saw land ahead.

"Can we pass them before we dock?" she yelled nervously over the snapping of the sails. The wind had increased considerably during the night.

"I'm sure we can. Hold onto the wheel while I reef the mainsail." He hurried forward and tightened the sail. Lacey could see their rival skipper at the helm of his boat. Cynthia was still missing, though, and she wondered if Rodney had pushed her into the ocean.

Preston came and took the wheel from her. "I can't sleep, so there's no need to take over for me."

"Could I get you something?"

"Coffee would be nice." He turned to her. "I think we're going to do it, Lacey."

Lacey went below and wondered what he'd do if they didn't. She started the water boiling and began to tidy the cabin, making up the bunks, putting her personal belongings in one place rather than scattered throughout the cabin, and straightening up the food supplies. Anything to keep herself busy. When the water had heated, she took him a large mug of coffee.

The dock soon came into focus, and Preston could see Cynthia languidly sunbathing on the deck of the *Filthy Rich*, seemingly unconcerned with the excitement of the race, and definitely not helping Rodney sail. Lacey stood beside Preston, nervously twirling her hair with her fingers. She could see individuals on the dock now, yet they were still a boat length behind the *Filthy Rich*.

Lacey wanted to scream, she felt so helpless. There was absolutely nothing either of them could do, to go any faster. Her palms were sweating and she crossed her arms in vexation.

Preston looked down at her. "Nervous?"

She nodded. "I wish there was something I could do. I hate being helpless."

"I've seen closer races than this. We still have a good chance. The finish line is at the large sloop outside the marina."

The *Stud Muffin* was edging up next to the *Filthy Rich* and Lacey could feel her heart beating in her ears. When they finally reached the sloop, the *Filthy Rich* was still in the lead, though by less than two feet. The gun sounded, and a cheer went up for Rodney and Cynthia. The *Stud Muffin* slid slowly into her slip at the marina, and Lacey was appalled at the pallor of Preston's face. As soon as they touched the pilings, she leaped off and forced her way through the crowds towards Cynthia and Rodney. Preston quickly tied up the boat and followed her.

After Lacey elbowed her way through the crowd to Rodney Fleming, to the astonishment of everyone, she kicked him swiftly in the groin with all her might.

"You lousy son-of-a-bitch! You heard my distress signal, and you sailed right by. You don't deserve to win, Rodney Fleming. Preston could have drowned for all you cared." Lacey was screaming at Rodney, who was doubled-up on the dock, as the crowd quickly became silent.

Preston backed away, ashamed he hadn't beat Lacey to the punch. As he eased his way through the crowd, he decided that more than anything right now, he needed a drink. He located Henry's estate wagon, and eased it out of the parking lot and headed for the Jolly Roger. Lacey obviously could take care of herself, and didn't need him.

The judges had joined the crowd on the dock, and were quickly informed of what had taken place. Cynthia was the first to speak when the three judges approached them all.

"I'd like to put forth a motion that the *Filthy Rich* be disqualified per Article 58, failure to render assistance."

The taller man looked astounded. "What happened?"

"We passed the *Stud Muffin* three days out from Bermuda and they sounded a distress signal during Mr. Fleming's watch. When I finally got on deck, I could see the other boat, but Mr. Fleming refused to turn back, or let me radio in a reading for the Coast Guard. In fact, he ripped out the radio." She glared down at Rodney.

Lacey was still breathing heavily over Rodney's prostrate figure. Slowly, Cynthia's recitation of the facts registered with her and someone had to restrain her as she went to kick Rodney again.

"Is this true, Ms. Campbell?" the taller judge asked Lacey.

"Yes. If Preston hadn't been wearing yellow foul weather gear, I'd never have found him." She tried not to sound hysterical, but the fear she had felt that day was obvious in her voice.

Someone had helped Rodney stand up and he looked ready to kill both Cynthia and her.

"Mr. Fleming, have you anything to add?" asked one of the judges.

Rodney began calling Lacey and Cynthia a string of names until the crowd pulled him away and took him to his boat.

"If both of you will come to the yacht club office tomorrow and swear out affidavits, we'll declare the *Stud Muffin* the winner, officially."

Both Cynthia and Lacey nodded, and the crowds slowly dispersed. Cynthia held out her hand to Lacey. "Congratulations. Preston and you deserved to win, anyway. Rodney is such an ass. I'm sorry I couldn't help you. I wanted to."

"You did help." Lacey stood on her tiptoes and looked frantically for Preston. "Where did Preston get to?"

Cynthia shook her head. "Sorry. All I could see was Rodney writhing in pain. I better get my stuff off his boat before he tosses it overboard."

Lacey stood a moment longer, letting the fact that they had won the race slowly sink in. She let out a whoop that made several heads turn in her direction, before sprinting back to the *Stud Muffin.*

"Preston!" She jumped on deck, almost sliding off the other side of the boat. She ran down the companionway. "Preston!" She stopped and frowned. He wasn't on the boat. She gathered her gear and waited anxiously on deck, sitting on her duffel bag.

She saw Henry running down the pier, and she looked for Preston to be with him, but he was alone. He leaped on board and swung Lacey around dangerously close to the water.

"You won! I knew it! Where's Preston?"

"I thought you knew." She bit her lip. "His stuff's

still here, but I haven't seen him since we docked. He doesn't even know we won."

"Where could he be?" Henry looked as puzzled as she felt. "Come on. I'll take you to a hotel, and then I'll go to the Rockwell place and see if he's there. He probably wanted a shower or something."

"Will you bring him to me and let me tell him?"

"Of course. Any preference as to a hotel?"

"Yes." She named the one where she had met Preston a little over two weeks ago. "It's my lucky hotel," she added. A shower would feel good and she'd like to clean up before seeing Preston again.

Henry took her to pick up her bags at the bus station and left her at the hotel after taking her bags inside for her. She showered and dressed in a bright Hawaiian print sundress and sandals. After an hour, she called information for Preston's phone number, but was informed by the operator that the phone had been disconnected over two weeks ago. Lacey let the receiver slide quietly into the cradle and sat heavily on the bed.

Finally she called her mother.

"Where are you?" was her mother's first question.

Lacey gave the name and number of the hotel.

"Was it a nice trip?"

"It was wonderful. I may take up sailing."

"Are you coming home?" her mother asked hopefully.

"No. I like it here," she answered quickly.

"I have some news." Her mother sounded hesitant.

"What? Are you okay?"

"I'm fine, but Jodi's pregnant. We just found out."

"Oh great! Frank wanted children right away."

"You're not upset?"

"No. Not really. Tell them I'm happy for them."

"You sound like you mean it," her mother said in wonder.

"I do, Mom. I'm fine, now. I don't think I ever really loved Frank, anyway." Or at least she had certainly never felt towards Frank what she felt towards Preston.

Her mother laughed. "You sound great, honey. I miss you. A husband isn't the same as having a daughter to talk to."

"I miss you, too. Tell everyone hello for me and I'll call you tomorrow." They hung up. Lacey's stomach growled, and she decided to go down and get some dinner. She left a message at the front desk in case Preston or Henry called, and headed for the dining room by way of the bar. Even in the half light, she spotted Preston as soon as she walked in.

He was sitting at the bar, forlornly staring at a huge frozen margarita that had melted long ago. She slipped up behind him and hugged his neck.

"Where did you go so fast?" she whispered in his ear.

Preston was startled. He hadn't expected her to find him. He couldn't bring himself to look at her. "To lick my wounds. I'm so sorry, Lacey."

She perched on the stool next to him. "For what?" she asked brightly, grabbing a pretzel from the bowl in front of him.

"For losing, for leading you on, for promising you money I don't have." He looked down at the bar and swirled his glass in the puddle it had made.

"You have money."

"No, I don't. In fact I owe you two thousand, five

hundred dollars. I owe Henry five thousand. Then there's eighty-eight thousand in late payments due on our estate, not to mention the hundred thousand I need to pay the mortgage off. They've threatened foreclosure next month."

"Will two hundred thousand cover everything?" Lacey nonchalantly munched on another pretzel.

"Very funny."

"We won, Preston."

"Lacey, you're dreaming."

"You didn't hang around to hear what Cynthia said to the judges. She told on Rodney, but good. Tomorrow we're going to the Yacht Club to swear out affidavits against him, and they'll present us with a check then."

"Are you serious?" Preston looked at her in disbelief.

Lacey looked at him seriously. "Would I lie about something this important to you?"

Preston looked into her clear green eyes. "We actually won?"

Lacey threw down her half-eaten pretzel. "Gee whiz, Preston, what do I have to do to convince you?"

"We won!" he hollered, lifting her off the bar stool.

Several heads turned their way, but Preston didn't care. He kissed her for all he was worth, and it wasn't until the applause of the other bar patrons filtered through to him that he released a flushed and dazed Lacey.

"Wow!" was all she could say.

He hugged her tightly and kissed the top of her head. "We couldn't have won without you, Lacey. After I straighten out the mortgage on my mom's house, and get a job, a real job, I want to see you, date you, be with you."

Lacey pushed away. "I'm not waiting for you to do all that, Preston Rockwell. It's now or never."

He looked at her and saw a glimmer of determination in her eyes. "What do you mean?"

"It's now or never. I've put my life on hold too many times. No more waiting."

He cleared his throat as he realized her implication. "Are you so sure of everything?"

"As sure as most people are, and as I can be."

"Shouldn't we wait?"

"For what? What will change? Your feelings for me?"

He smiled. "No, I don't think so. You are so different than anyone I've ever known."

"Do you want to risk my feelings changing?"

He laughed. "No, I guess not. But just what are your feelings?"

"First, I want to know what yours are."

He leaned down and kissed her again, slowly, deeply, and completely. When he stopped, they were both shaken by the intensity of the feelings they had kept under control since the night they had made love.

"Okay, that's out of the way. Lacey, would you like to form a permanent partnership?"

"Oh, Preston." She fluttered her eyes at him demurely. "This is so sudden! I've only known you for two weeks."

"Listen, woman, you know more about me in two weeks than anyone has ever known about me. It's been an intense, um, experience."

"Ummmm. Okay, I'll be your partner on one condition."

Preston sat heavily back on his barstool. "I have a funny feeling I've just fallen into a trap of some kind," he sighed. "Go ahead."

"I want you to help me open a restaurant." He looked ready to protest, but she held up her hand to silence him. "We could get a small business loan. I know what to do and I know we could make a go of it."

He felt himself get all warm at her saying "we" so naturally, and she seemed to think he could actually contribute to the success of such a venture.

"Do you really think we can run a restaurant?"

"I have the utmost confidence in us as a team, don't you?" she answered blithely.

"Yes, I do. Can you wait for an engagement ring?"

"Forget the ring. I'd rather have a Silver King 5000 industrial size refrigerator-freezer anyway."

"What about a big wedding?"

"I'd rather have a Jet Stream Model 210 combination grill, stove and oven, plus real cloth napkins and tablecloths, and a patio built for outside dining at our restaurant."

"We really won, didn't we?" Preston gathered her against him and hugged her tightly.

"Ouch! For Pete's sake! We won already. Put me down. People are staring at us!"

"I'm going to go home, take a shower, call my mother, and tomorrow, after we get the check, I'll straighten out the mortgage problem, and settle my debts."

"No," Lacey said firmly.

"What do you mean, no?"

"I mean you aren't leaving me here. You can do all that just as well with me as without me. Besides, after the visit to the bank, we're going to look for a place for our restaurant downtown."

"Are you really serious about that?"

"Maybe. Maybe not," she said impishly. "Maybe we should open a gourmet bakery instead. And we could call it—"

"Oh, no. Not that," Preston said, alarmed.

"Oh, yes. *The Stud Muffin.*"

Suddenly he swept her up in his arms and carried her off to the elevator. Lacey unwrapped an arm from around his neck, reached down to press the button, and kissed him.

"Where are you taking me?"

"The honeymoon suite."

"Did you reserve it?"

"No."

"Are you going to pick the lock? Are you crazy?"

"Yes." Preston grinned. "Crazy about you. And ready to get started in the happy-ever-after stuff."

Lacey kissed him again, and sighed with joy.

"Me, too."